The Water War Episode I

Shirley Johnson

Any resemblance of characters to anyone living or dead is purely coincidental.

This is a work of fiction.

ISBN:
ISBN-13:

DEDICATION

To my husband Craig who always encourages me to be creative and always lets me have time to daydream and write.

ACKNOWLEDGMENTS

Shawn Crapo aka Edward Crae wouldn't take this idea of mine for a dystopian novel, so I finally wrote it myself and I thank him for turning it down. I've had a lot of fun getting out of my box and writing something 'different'.

The Water War

Episode I

Shirley Johnson

CHAPTER ONE

She stocked up on everything. Especially on her favorite things. The things she liked to have plenty of such as canned chili and Tums and toilet paper. She always worried for just a moment what the check-out guy would think of her. She worried just for a moment, for as long as it took her to get to the water aisle and then she didn't worry any longer. Because then she was calculating. Water and gallons and days and years and that would lead her to the emergency first aid and bandages and batteries and matches and lanterns and sometimes she'd splurge and pick up something like a camouflage jacket or a tent. But the tent ended up giving her anxiety. The tent meant that she was planning on a time when she would need to leave her home.

She regretted buying the tent. But not the rain barrels.

She had four rain barrels. One on each corner of her house. And she checked them daily. Checked them for leaks. Checked them for algae. Checked them to check them. She checked them with her tape measure. She had to tell herself to not record the inches in them. But she always did, but only after a rainstorm. The date and the inches of rain.

She loved the rain barrels more than she loved her pool. The pool was a source of anxiety as well because she worried constantly that the neighbors were going to comment about it. Like why she never got in it. And why she never had them over to swim.

The pool was supposed to have been a source of calm. She'd felt complete calm if not an excited calm the first time she'd seen it at the super store. But it'd brought anxiety as soon as she got it put up and filled with water.

It's a wonder it hadn't given her anxiety when she had to ask an employee to help her get it out to her car. And it was a wonder it hadn't caused her anxiety when she had to get it from her car to the back yard. But she had done it with determination.

But the pool was permanent. No taking it back. No taking it down. It was there pumping and filtering 7000 gallons of water every day. She caught herself staring at the pool noodles on the end cap in the super store. No need for one of those. She would not be getting in her water.

She pushed her cart full of can goods and water bottles and bandaids and batteries to the front of the store and was only distracted from heading to the register when the rack of seeds caught her eye. There she pondered packet after packet comparing green beans to green beans. Who knew there were so many kinds of green beans?

"Are you putting in a garden?" a man asked her and Ernestine looked up to see the sun burnt face of her neighbor, Pete.

"No," she said as she turned the green bean packet over in her small black hands. "But I should," she added as an afterthought.

"Heck of a drought going on right now, though," Pete said and looked up at the sky lights in the rafters of the barebones ceiling in the super store.

"Yes," Ernestine agreed though her voice was flat, "Heck of a drought."

"Did you know you can grow potatoes in a stack of car tires?" Pete asked her and stroked his short blonde beard.

Ernestine stood there for twenty minutes while Pete explained how you could grow potatoes in old tires. That afternoon she booked an appointment to bring her car back in and get new tires on the Prius. She couldn't help but shop for ten more gallons of water while she waited for her car to be done. Ten more gallons was at least ten more days of life. If she was careful. If it came down to it.

"Be sure to put the old tires in the hatchback," she told the mechanic as she opened a gallon of spring water and drank right from the large jug.

CHAPTER TWO

"What's the weather doing there?"

"Dry, hot. There?"

"Same."

"Price of gas?"

"Buck Ninety," Ernestine's mother answered her on the phone. Her lips sounded dry.

They had this conversation nearly every night.

"How much is gas there?" her mother asked her.

"Dollar eighty-five last time I was out."

There was silence on the phone for a few seconds while they decided what the next topic would be.

"It was 98 out this afternoon," her mom told her.

"Hmph."

Ernestine always felt like her mom was trying to compete with her with the temperatures and no matter what Ernestine said, she always felt as if she were losing the competition.

"What was it there today?" her mom finally asked when she didn't offer up a response.

"78."

"Hmph. It was 98 here."

"Ayuh, but you're in the desert, mom."

"Yes, but it's only April. 98 in April. What's it gonna be in May?"

"I don't know," sighed Ernestine.

She wished her mom would move out of the desert and would move in with her. Her mom was the only one who knew about her water. She had seen it the last time she'd visited and she'd agreed it was a good idea. And she'd even gone with Ernestine to buy more.

"They can go to war all they want over oil, and power, and God too for that matter," her mom had said as she ran a finger down one of the deep creases in her seventy-six year old face that had darkened to a deep onyx color from years of living in the desert sun. "But we wouldn't last long without plain old water. 'Specially where I live!" she'd added on at the end just as her pale green eyes connected with Ernestine's own. She understood. And that's why it was ok for Ernestine to ask her now, "How much water cost there?"

"Buck ninety-nine a gallon."

"As much as gas," Ernestine said thoughtfully.

"Ayuh," came from her mom. "And there?"

"Dollar thirty-eight."

"Hmph well our drought's worse than yours."

"Yes. But ours could get bad too. Been two months since we had rain."

Ernestine's dark eyes sparkled in the dim light of the kitchen. She liked to talk about the drought and the rains and the prices of things with her mother. It eased her anxiety. It gave her some insight to what her mom was stocking up on without asking her outright. A person's hoard was private.

That and neither one wanted the government listening in to know what they were doing and they both swore the government was listening in.

Ernestine ended the conversation when the news came on. She sat back in her leather recliner and listened about a shortage on .22 LR ammo. Personally, she couldn't see why people were in a panic over a shortage in .22 ammo. But she was interested in the protesting and the panic that was taking place across the nation. She was intrigued at the outrage on people's faces as the news showed the lines and the mobs of angry people, almost all of them were men. Men in camouflage. It made her think of her coat she'd bought. What did she share in common with them, she wondered. It made her think of her ex-husband. She wondered if he was hoarding ammo still.

It seemed as if a national debate were heating up about gun ammo in general and not just the .22 caliber. Masses of people were chanting that the government was stockpiling all the ammo for themselves. And politicians were screaming right back at them that they were the ones stockpiling the ammo.

The politicians threatened to pass stricter gun control laws and were already enforcing executive orders on limits of how much ammo one person could buy. There were talks of databases and background checks on purchases. The gun owners threatened to make their own bullets and to revolt against the government. The politicians threatened to outlaw lead bullets altogether because they said lead was bad for the environment. One senator claimed that it wasn't just the cause of cancer but that it was also the cause of climate change and maybe even the cause of the current drought the entire nation was suffering from.

The fight went on and on and the news covered both sides ad nauseum but Ernestine was no longer hearing any of it. Her ears had start ringing when she heard database and restrictions on limits. Her imagination went into full panic and she feared and imagined the superstore keeping track of all the water she had bought over the years.

She came back to the present when she heard the newscaster say a special report was coming up next on people who hoard guns and other things to prepare for the end of the world. Ernestine didn't see why you'd hoard guns and ammo. In the end all you'd need was water, really.

She shook her head to herself as she padded into the kitchen to make popcorn and as the oil began to heat up in the pan on the stove, she fished out her buyers card from her wallet, the one she presented at the superstore for special savings and coupons every time she went. And as her popcorn began to pop, she cut up the little plastic card and burned it in the cast iron skillet. They wouldn't track how much water she'd be buying nor anything else in the future. She wouldn't be in any database.

CHAPTER THREE

"Those are illegal now," her neighbor Pete said to her and pointed at the blue rain barrel.

She hadn't wanted to have him over to her backyard. She knew nothing but trouble would come from it and here it was.

"What?" she asked him in a panic.

"Rain barrels," he said and nodded towards the rain barrel as she flipped on the spigot on the bottom of it and filled a gallon jug with water for the potatoes Pete was showing her how to plant in her tires.

"Why are rain barrels illegal?" she asked and then said, "When did that happen?"

She watched the news religiously and read the paper every morning cover to cover and hadn't seen that.

"It passed in DC 'bout four days ago," Pete shrugged. "They call it 'Rainwater Harvesting'. They said that a state's water rights extend to the drops that fall on your roof and that it's called natural resource appropriation." Pete shrugged and stroked his beard.

"What will they do if you have one?"

She waited for him to answer while he wiped dirt off the blade of the spade with his bare fingers. The sun glinted off the gold frames of his glasses while he bowed his head.

"Well, I don't know," he finally answered. "I guess the news said the barrels aren't illegal themselves, but collecting water in them now is."

Ernestine thought that over for a minute, her mind chasing the thought around and around like a tired dog chasing its own tail.

"They're like the bongs of water control," Pete said and chuckled and wiped his glasses off on his shirt tail.

"What do you mean?" Ernestine asked.

"Well, you can own one but you better not put anything in it," he said and laughed.

Ernestine's thoughts went to her private stash she grew in the back corner of her lot amongst the sunflowers. She had to get Pete out of her yard. She didn't know where he stood on things. Was he a do-gooder who would tell on her or was he someone who bucked the law? Either way, she'd be relieved when he went home.

That night she surfed the internet for all the news she could find on the outlawing of rain barrels but didn't find much till she typed in Pete's term of 'rainwater harvesting'. Then she found several articles but nothing from the perspective of the citizen. All she could find were articles and reports of politicians basically clapping each other on the back congratulating each other for taking the water rights right out of the sky.

There was nothing about it on tv, on the ten o'clock news, or in the paper. She flicked from station to station from where she sat on the edge of her rocker with a mason jar of water in her hand. She startled and nearly dropped it when the phone rang.

"Well?" her mother asked instead of hello.

"Well?" she asked back.

"I haven't seen you on the message boards."

The message boards on Amazon's website was where Ernestine's mom spent most of her nights. She liked to review things and she liked to ask questions about things and she had built a huge amount of friends and enemies as well, on the message boards, the community boards, and the review pages.

"I've been busy."

"Doing what?" she asked but didn't wait for an answer. "Mighty dry out these days," her mother said in a tight, wise old voice. The know it all voice that waited patiently for Ernestine to clue in.

"What's that mean?"

"You seen the news the other day?" her mom asked.

"No, I seem to have missed it." She knew just what her mom was talking about.

"You've heard though, haven't ya?"

"About the rain barrels?" Ernestine asked.

"Shhhhh, yes," her mom hushed her.

"Shhh?"

"Yes. Don't say it out loud."

"Why?"

"I think the government is listening. I think they flag certain conversations, certain words," her mother whispered.

They had always joked that the government was listening and Ernestine always thought about it like how you think about a far off fear. Yes it was scary to imagine, but it was not really real. But now it felt very real. She felt the hair on her neck prickle with sweat and she looked behind her where she was standing in the kitchen, as if she expected to see men in suits standing there.

"Oh," was all Ernestine said.

"Yes, oh. So what are you going to do about it, Ernestine?" It was the same old voice she'd used on her her whole life whenever she was in a pickle and her mother was waiting to see if she could get out of it on her own.

"Nothing," Ernestine said after a few seconds of thinking.

"That's my girl. How hot did it get there today?"

And they were back with their competition.

"I don't know," Ernestine said in a far away voice. She felt uncertain of where she was even standing much less what the weather did today. And finally she told her mom, "80, it was 80 today."

"80 in Illinois in April. That's pretty warm."

"Yep."

"100 here. 100 in Utah in April. Gonna be brutal this summer."

"No rain for two months."

"I don't even recall the last rain here," said her mom, always winning the competition.

Ernestine heard her mom take a long drink. She imagined how hot and dry it was down there.

"You should move up here with me," she told her.

"Air's too moist for my asthma. And too cold in the winter. You should move down here where it's warm."

Ernestine could say too hot, too dry down there but the truth was she liked the heat. The truth was she just did not want to leave her home. She'd lived there eight years. Eight years of trying to make a family and trying to save a marriage. It held a lot of failed memories and a lot of loneliness. And now it held a lot of water. She could never leave. Especially never leave all her water for the desert.

It was as if her mother read her mind.

"I have enough water for the two of us. Should we need it," she added on the end.

"I'll think about it," Ernestine promised her and she meant it.

Living in the house with all that water was sometimes starting to feel suffocating. She felt it pulling on her when she left the house. She felt as if she was sitting on top of something alive; waiting for some battle that never began. She felt the bottles and bottles of water pulling her down when she went next door to Pete's to ask a question about the potatoes. She felt the weight of all that water pulling her back to her house; to count it, to check on it, to get more.

The pool had looked beautiful in the sun when she walked back over to her own yard and for the first time she was tempted to get in it. But she didn't.

CHAPTER FOUR

Flip-Flop went the mail slot.

"WE'RE COMING TO YOUR NEIGHBORHOOD!" the post card said in huge cheerful capital letters. It was from the water company and it told Ernestine that she needed to call them and schedule a time for the water company to come put a new meter on her main line down in the basement.

"What's this all about?" she asked the cheerful woman on the line when she called the 800 number on the post card.

"Oh we're updating our system to give you a better rate on your water. We'd also like to schedule a consultation with all our customers on how to make their homes more water efficient, to show our appreciation for your valued business."

Ernestine tamped down the panic she was feeling and made the appointment for next week for a water employee to put a meter on her pipes. She told the chipper girl she'd have to call back about the efficiency consultation.

Ernestine stood in the kitchen shifting her weight from foot to foot as her mind raced on how to get that water man out of her house as fast as possible. It would require another trip to the super store.

Later that afternoon, wearing a bandana over her nose and mouth, Ernestine poured little dollops of pure ammonia into the five litter boxes she'd filled with cheap cat litter, in her basement.

She shut the door firmly behind her when she came upstairs and peeled off her gloves. Next she sat out seven cat food bowls but kept them empty for now, and went outside to check on her rain barrels. All four barrels held only about eight inches of water each. It smelled green and dark when she filled up a watering can to water her potato plants she was trying to grow. The dirt was dry and had deep cracks in it. The grass in her yard looked dried out and dusty. Yet the pool rippled happily in the sun and she shut her eyes and sighed when she stuck her arm in it to pull out the thermometer. 85 degrees. The water was very warm for April.

"Beautiful day to swim," Pete called over the fence.

She pulled her arm out and shook it off and went back in the house with his eyes prickling on the back of her head. She had things to do; she unbraided all her hair and put the comb on the stove burner to heat it up and a million memories of her mom doing her hair before picture day swam in front of her eyes as she prepared to make herself invisible to the water man.

The day before the water man came was a long one; one of spending most of it on the toilet with a very upset stomach. First of all Ernestine was upset because he was coming. And secondly she was upset because of something her mother had told her.

"You have to put quarters in to take a shower," her mom had told her the night before.

Ernestine didn't know what to say, so she sat quiet.

"Did you hear me? Quarters to take a shower," she said firmer.

"Are you exaggerating? Is that real?" Ernestine asked.

"It's real. I'm staring right at it. The water company came out and put controllers on my pipes. I can only use so many gallons a day for warshing and flushing and drinking and now I have to feed quarters into a timer for showering."

"I don't believe it."

"Well believe it. I'll load a picture of it up tonight. Go look at it, you'll see. Look for it under my reviews on the boards tonight."

"I will," Ernestine said quietly. She couldn't believe what her mother was saying about a timer and quarters on her shower but yet she knew her mom to always be down to earth and to never exaggerate even if she did always seem to win the competition of who had worse weather.

"You even remember my user name?"

"Yes, mom."

"What are you gonna do if they install that on your shower?"

"I don't know. I'll figure something out."

"Figure something out for me now and don't be away from the boards so long," she said and hung up with a far away click.

The boards. Her mother was constantly reviewing things she never bought, on Amazon. And she refused to use email so if she had something to show Ernestine she uploaded or typed it up to look like a review on Amazon and had Ernestine look it up. No wonder Ernestine was paranoid. And no wonder she couldn't get off the toilet today. Maybe her water company man was coming to put one of those coin operated timers on her shower.

In between trips to the pot she tried to get ready for the visit from the water man. She hung towels drenched in ammonia over oscillating fans in the front room and let them blow the stink throughout her house. She could barely breathe and had to open her windows as she worked hard to move all her water from one section of the basement to the other so that the water man wouldn't see them when he came.

The smell that night was so bad, and her nerves were so ramped up she couldn't sleep. Especially after she went on the boards and saw the picture of the long metal box with the wind up knob on it and the slot for quarters which was now welded to her mother's shower.

This picture had upset her so badly that she had spent the late hours of the night on her back porch smoking her pipe and trying to relax as she lay back in her canvas chair. She kept stealing paranoid glances over at Pete's house. It'd be just like him to come over all bright eyed and bushy tailed at 3am, wanting to chat or swim or smoke with her.

Ernestine pulled her thin black legs up under her and laughed and coughed out a plume of smoke at the thought of the two of them swimming in her pool in the middle of the night.

Ernestine woke up with the birds singing as she slept in the canvas chair on the back porch with an empty pipe still in her hands. She quickly gathered up her bag and her lighter and her things and went inside to change.

The water man was prompt at 8 and he could not stop staring at Ernestine in her pink sweat suit that had cat faces silkscreened on every inch of it. She had also braided her long hair into two plaits and had on flip flops with rainbow striped socks. She even had two little plastic barrettes in her hair that had cats on them. The water man visibly flinched when he came in the front door and was assailed with all the ammonia.

"Have many cats?" he asked as he covered his nose with a hanky and headed through the house as she led the way to the basement.

"Oh not many," she smiled as they walked past the seven food bowls with remnants of stinky tuna in them. She didn't offer him a number; let him guess how many cats she had hiding in the house.

He did his job in the basement quickly; the stench down there amongst the boxes dribbled with ammonia was even stronger, and he left without a word.

Let him put in her record that she was a crazy cat lady who was harmlessly nuts.

As soon as his van was gone, she went to work cleaning up and airing out the house; mopping the floors and taking a shower, and throwing away the cat covered jogging suit in the trash. But then she had second thoughts and dug it back out and threw it in the wash. A good way to be invisible was to be black and to look crazy. People discounted the mentally ill. She knew that first hand.

"Any idea on how to fix my shower?" her mom asked her that night as she was baking a Hungry Man frozen dinner of fish and chips and cherry cobbler in the oven. They were microwavable but the microwave just didn't get them crispy like she liked them.

"Can you pry it off?" Ernestine asked her as she peeked in the oven door at her dinner and its bubbling contents.

"No. It's welded on and there's a warning in some paperwork I had to sign giving them permission to put it on that says punishable up to fifty years in prison for tampering with it."

"You had to give them written permission to do that to your shower?"

"Yes."

"Why'd you give it to them?"

"I don't know. I felt afraid."

"Afraid?"

"You should have seen them."

"There was more than one guy?"

"There were three. They were all over the house, Ernie. They looked like cops. It was frightening."

Ernestine's nerves were raw that night as she ate her hot dinner and watched the news from all over the nation; all of which was unsettling. California was experiencing the worst draught of the decade. Fires were blazing across the entire southern portion of the state. Forests and homes and highways were being eaten up by flames that knew no boundary. You could literally watch the fire crawl from house to house on live tv. The state was having a hard time finding enough water to fight the fires and everyone was on water rationing in the entire state.

Then down in Texas and up in Michigan two towns' water supplies were found to be heavily tainted with lead; so much so that children were experiencing irreversible brain damage. Citizens and politicians pointed fingers at each other as to who was to blame while the president declared it a disaster.

While down in Arkansas, Oklahoma and Alabama people were showing news reporters how they could light their tap water on fire as it came out of the faucet. Groups marched and protested and blamed it on fracking and dangerous over-mining.

Environment groups near Ernestine's own town marched on the tv news as they blew the whistle on factories for storing CO2 underground, saying that not only was it poisoning the water supply it was also a ticking time bomb that could blow up and suffocate everyone with in a 25 mile radius.

Ernestine's arm froze mid scoop in her cherry cobbler as she watched, listened, and learned that underneath the outskirts of her own city, poisonous gas was buried in highly pressurized containers below the bedrock to keep it from polluting the sky as they processed soybeans and made everything from bacon bits to dog treats.

The national news continued on how in Louisiana, Mississippi, and Florida hundreds of people were ill and hundreds more had died from amoeba infested water that they had swam in to get relief from the heat.

"It ate him alive from the inside out!" a woman wailed into the camera as nurses covered her bloated husband up with a sheet in the background and they carted him out of the hospital room.

While up in Minnesota an entire camp of cub scouts were hospitalized and all in comas from flesh eating bacteria they had come in contact with while camping and canoeing upstate in the Boundary Waters. Parents wept on live tv that their sons would all be severely disabled after multiple amputations if they lived at all.

"Officials are urging everyone to boil their water before consuming as hospitals nationwide struggle to admit and care for all of these emergencies that broke out in the past twenty-four hours," the reporter ended the broadcast with a somber look on her face.

"Have you seen the news yet?" Ernestine had dialed her mom as quick as she could.

"No, it's early here still."

So Ernestine filled her mom in on what was happening around the country.

"The country is going to hell," was all her mom could say.

"It's finally happening just like I knew it would."

"I told you it would."

"You did." And she was right, it was Ernestine's mom who had always told her this would come. And now she was right.

"Aww, it'll pass. Things like this come and go. They'll get it straightened out, Ernie. They always do," her mom told her and tried to calm her down before hanging up.

All the same, Ernestine knew her mom would get right on the boards as soon as she hung up, to connect with other paranoids in the country and see what was happening.

Ernestine herself got on the boards that night and reviewed a rubber hose and shower head and tagged her mother's user name in the review for her to see. Her mom could hook that up to the sink which didn't have the coin operated timer on it. Her mom could shower from a hose in the sink. That was a little better. So long as the water wasn't infested with amoeba or bacteria or lead or just plain out flammable.

Ernestine was thankful the super store was open twenty-four hours because that night she went and bought two carts worth of water and all the fifths of Jack Daniels that they had, which was thirty-five bottles. She was going to need a drink when she tried to catch her tap water on fire. She felt like she could foresee a day when she would need a lot of drinks.

When she got home she was too tired to carry in the water and left all but one bottle of Jack Daniels in the car to bring in the next day. She took the one bottle of Jack straight to the kitchen and poured herself two fingers worth in a small Mason jar and went out on the back porch with her little bag of things and her pipe.

She swore she wasn't going to try to light the sink water on fire. She didn't want to know if it were flammable. But after drinking several gulps of the warm liquid and getting her pipe filled but not lighting it, she went back into the kitchen with her lighter.

She felt like a fool for trying to light the water. All that happened was she got her arm soaked and ruined a good lighter. She threw the lighter away on her way out back and grabbed another one out of the junk drawer before heading out onto the porch. She lit her pipe and as she inhaled the dark sharp smelling smoke, she laughed at herself for trying to light the sink water. What a ridiculous thought; that she could light her sink water on fire just because she saw it on the news. It had to have been fake. She smoked her pipe and sipped her Jack and sat back in the canvas chair in the warm night and stared out at the clear dark and the bright stars.

"You know something I don't?" Ernestine heard from behind her as she was unloading the two carts worth of bottled water from the back of her Prius the next day.

It was her neighbor, Pete.

He grinned at her from under the scorching noon sun and tucked his long blonde hair behind his ears and came towards her.

"Let me help you carry all that in. You look tired, anyhow," he said and began helping her carry all the water to the basement.

She let him see all the water in the back of her car. And then she let him see all the bottles of Jack. His eyebrows went up on his forehead a little but he didn't say a word.

She let him come in the house and she hoped the smell of ammonia was gone. She let him follow her downstairs. She felt her heart hammering under the buttons of her work shirt as she heard him clomp down the broad stairs behind her. She bit her lip and knew there was no turning back. She let him see her supplies.

"You won't tell?" Ernestine finally spoke to him after they had carried down five trips worth of water and all the clinking bottles of whiskey and added them to the shelves already stacked high.

"Hey, it's cool," Pete said and held both hands up to her as he stepped back a pace and looked at all of her supplies. It was mostly water.

The basement was divided into two rooms. The first room was 15x22. It had a fireplace and her washer and dryer, a sink and a couch and chair. The second room was 22x30 and the ceiling was much lower. That was where she kept her water. It took up half the room. Gallon jugs on one side and small water bottles in cases on the other. A quarter of the room was stacked with canned goods on homemade shelves six inches off the ground. They were having a drought but it was possible they would have a flood someday and she didn't want her canned goods sitting in a swamp.

"You're ready for it," Pete said.

"For what?" she asked. She wanted him to put a name to it. To what was coming.

Pete was quiet with his hands on his hips as he leaned back a bit and looked at all the food, the matches, the batteries, the bandaids, the chili, the instant pudding, the fire starter sticks, the lighters, the flares, and the water. All that water.

"What am I ready for?" she asked him, her voice barely a whisper.

"For the zombie apocalypse," he laughed.

She didn't answer but she felt her face burning with embarrassment.

"Or at least for the water war," he said much more seriously.

"Yes, the water war," she echoed and when she looked at him she couldn't see his eyes through his lenses for the reflections of the ceiling light; all she could see were two pale circles and for a moment she felt a chill run up her neck.

**

CHAPTER FIVE

Ernestine hated, absolutely hated not understanding a thing immediately. She was relatively bright and very resourceful and when she didn't understand something immediately, when she couldn't learn something from the first glance, or first try, it enraged her so furiously she saw red. And when she was furious she was apt to hurt herself accidentally. She was forever burning herself or spilling something hot on her hands or cutting her fingers with a dull knife. When she was working at something that she was too weak to unscrew or hammer or she was too uncoordinated to make something work, she would hammer at it till she hurt her knuckles or got skinned up so bad that tears would well up in her eyes.

She was feeling this way right now.

She wanted to learn how to reload bullets. She wanted a list of everything she would need. She liked lists. She liked clear step by step directions. But the how-to videos were long and boring and unorganized. She wanted the directions of how to reload bullets to be as clear cut as a recipe for a simple cake.

And then she found out she would need a special license just to buy the things she needed such as black powder.

She had spent the past two days all excited thinking she would teach herself how to reload bullets. That she would stock up on bullets. That bullets would be the currency of the future. But it wasn't that easy. It wasn't as easy as buying water. Collecting water. In the end she was so frustrated and so close to screaming and throwing things that she drove off to the superstore in her Prius as fast as she could go and she filled out the application for the firearm license and she decided she would start buying bullets as soon as she could. And maybe someday even a gun. The idea of a gun made her happy and she was still smiling when she got home. She was still smiling despite the fact that she had now put herself into one of the most watched databases of the federal government.

Her other neighbor Robert, froze that smile right off her face and left her teeth feeling bare as she stood in her drive.

Robert was her neighbor on the other side of her house, opposite of Pete. She knew he didn't like her. He always looked at her with a combination of pity and dislike. He thought she was mentally ill. She knew that was what he thought. She knew it was why he looked at her with pity. But he also disliked her. She knew that by how he scowled at her Prius every time she rolled silently up in it. She didn't know if he disliked her for her Prius or because she was a woman or because she was black or because she was unemployed or all of the above.

"You need glass pack exhausts on that thing so we can hear you coming," he had told her one time when she had pulled up in the drive and startled him as he did yard work next to her side of the house.

"Well, actually the Prius still wouldn't make any sound because it doesn't produce hardly any," and here he cut her off with a wave of his hand in which he held his hedge clippers still. He didn't want to hear anything about her car. The sight of it always caused a look of disgust to cross his face.

He now stood in the bright sun stroking his huge mustache as he watched her open the back hatch of her car. She hesitated before unloading her groceries. Today she had normal groceries and only four gallons of water instead of twenty, or forty, or one hundred.

"Awful hot out today," Robert said from behind her.

She turned and saw him in his cargo shorts and Hawaiian shirt just standing there flexing the calves of his freckled legs. He had a watering can in his hand today.

"Everything's drying up," he said to her. His eyes were pale under bushy eyebrows as he stared at her.

"I don't have much to water," she told him and swallowed and she hurried and carried in her groceries before he could say the inevitable, "Good day for a swim," that he always said. She beat him inside before he did.

That night she peeked out her bedroom windows and saw down into Robert's first floor bedroom. He was sitting on the edge of his bed with a large black barbell in his hand curling it up, his elbow on his knee. He was shirtless and she could see the glow of the television flicker over his face and bare chest. She stood completely motionless and watched his muscles flex in his chest and stomach while he curled the barbell twenty times.

Ernestine pulled her curtains shut.

But they felt flimsy against the night. Robert could look up and tell if her light was on. Could maybe even see her shadow through the light material. She found a thick green blanket high up in her closet; folded neatly and stored away and she got it down and hung it in front of the window. She liked the thickness of it between her and the glass outside.

She thought about hanging blankets in front of all her windows. But that might seem weird to someone. It might seem ok in the winter, to keep out the draft. But it wasn't winter now. It was unseasonably hot. Which reminded her, she hadn't heard from her mother in a few days.

She spun around in a panic and looked at the alarm clock. 10:35. It would be a lot earlier in Utah. She couldn't remember if Utah was mountain time or the same time as Arizona or what but she knew it was early enough to call.

"Mom, where you been?"

"Right here in the armpit of Utah. Right here in the desert. But been showering at the campground though."

Ernestine could hear the smile in her mother's voice.

"No limit on water at the campground. Can't decide if I should put that on the boards or not, let other people know."

"Why would you put that on the boards?"

"Why wouldn't I?" her mother cracked back at her. "It could be helpful to other folks in the same predicament as me."

Which was true. She put all of her other conspirator information and ideas on the Amazon boards; tucked amongst the reviews for blenders and Brita water filters and tents and wet start matches were where all the off the grid anti-government conspirators went to talk in secret.

Ernestine balanced in between feeling it was ridiculous to be afraid that the boards were being monitored by the government and feeling silly that hiding your ideas there was even necessary. Being monitored. She glanced at her windows in her upstairs hallway which were now all covered in old blankets. At least she couldn't be monitored upstairs, she thought to herself and missed something her mom said.

"You did what, Mom?"

"I said I needed another shower after I got home from the campground shower. It's so hot out my bike tires stuck to the tar."

"Why'd you bike? What's wrong with the truck?"

"Nothing's wrong with it. It's only a quarter mile to the KOA. That's not worth the gas. Plus I didn't want anyone seeing my truck there. I pulled my bike right into the ladies' room. But I was soaking wet by the time I biked home."

"What's the temp there?"

"105 yesterday. There?"

"79. And dry."

"Mhm. I biked to the Foxy after my shower just because I already had my bike out. And water's up. $2.79 a gallon. Course I couldn't get any anyway because I was on the bike and I don't like to put anything too heavy in the baskets."

Ernestine listened to her mother go on and on about normal things such as biking around the desert and cleaning her little mobile home out in the desert. It took her mind off water and blankets and her neighbor Robert who didn't like her.

**

"If you live in one of these four cities your drinking water is likely safe," the anchorman in the gray suit and yellow tie warned tv viewers on the ten o'clock news. There had been no warning of this startling news during the first fifteen minutes of the broadcast. There was no foretelling that such a thing would be discussed. It totally popped up without expectation and Ernestine nearly choked as she sipped her warm Jack Daniels.

"What?" she yelled at the tv as it went to commercial. "I didn't see! I didn't see which four cities!" she lamented at the set as an ad for a chiropractor blared at her. "Four cities?" she asked the dark living room.

Her heart pounded around in her chest and her pulse pounded in her ears and she shook her head to clear them. She found the remote for the DVR and hit record so she could rewatch it if she needed.

"In the whole United States? How can that be?"

She chewed the thick skin around her thumbnail as she waited for the news to come back on.

"Only four cities in the US can be trusted to not cheat on their water tests," the anchor Brock Andrews intoned straight into the camera as he leaned forward on his news desk. "I tell you Carol, if they cannot be trusted to protect little kids from lead in drinking water, what on earth can they be trusted with?" he asked the news lady next to him, the one with the over-sprayed bubble hair-do.

Carol sat there with a look of shock in her over-painted eyes.

"Who amongst us is safe?" Brock asked and smacked the desk, causing Carol to jump.

"What cities?" Ernestine demanded. "What cities?" she asked again as Carol told Brock to wait till he saw what the water was doing to people down in St. Louis.

"St Louis? That's only two hours away," Ernestine mumbled as the broadcast cut to a worried mom feeling the forehead of a red faced child with a sore throat.

Ernestine glugged down her Jack during a car insurance commercial and almost spit it out when the ad ended early and the news came back on. But the water story in St. Louis was only about the charitable trend sweeping the nation that summer as ice bucket challenges gripped the nation and raised money.

"Oh Carol," Brock Andrews chuckled, no residue of pinched concern evident on his face any longer. "What will they think of next?" he asked with such glee on his face that his dentures nearly fell out of his face. Ernestine imagined them hitting the hard surface of the desk and splintering into white crumbs. Would he say, "Oh Carol," then? Ernestine wondered.

"What four cities?" Ernestine howled as the news ended and then nearly jumped out of her skin as someone pounded on the door.

She stared between two gripped handfuls of curtain out onto the dark front porch to try to distinguish who it was but could only see a non-descript thick shape. And then it moved and she saw the moonlight glint off two lenses.

Pete.

"Pete? What do you want?" she asked through a small opening in the door.

"Let me in."

He had a hold of the storm door and was trying to wedge his foot in the opening of the big door.

"Why?"

"There's mosquitoes out here."

Ernestine let Pete in and they stood awkwardly for a couple of seconds before she finally offered him a seat on the low sofa.

"Did you see the news?" he asked and sounded excited.

"Why? What?"

"We're one of the cities they said."

"One of the four? I didn't see it, I missed it. We were one of the four?"

"Yeah, it's crazy, isn't it?"

"It's good. Isn't it?" Ernestine sounded hopeful.

"Hah."

"Hah?"

"Hah. Water here isn't safe, you know that."

"I do?"

"Yes," Pete said to her with doubt crumbling his eyebrows down. "It's why you hoard all that water."

"Our water's not safe?"

"Heck no."

"How do you know?"

Pete looked around the small room as if to make sure they weren't being over-heard.

"I looked at some samples," he told her as his eyebrows rose high up on his forehead. "After I saw all your water in the basement." Pete's voice sounded dry and papery and Ernestine doubted she was hearing what he was really saying.

She smacked herself on the side of the head three times like a swimmer will do when they get out of the pool and have water in their ear.

"Looked at it?" she asked.

"At work. At the lab."

Pete worked at the university. It would figure that he'd have his own lab.

"What's, what's wrong with it?" Ernestine cleared her throat and asked.

"Some lead, bacteria, organisms living in it that I haven't identified yet and lots of metals. A little iodine," he said as he held his hand out flat and tilted it one way and then the other.

"What can we do?" Ernestine asked, always ready to plan, always needing to take action, make lists, purchase things, get ready.

Pete rubbed his thin fingers together from where he sat on her couch and the sound made a chill run up her back and caused her to shiver.

"I'm doing more tests on it but I wouldn't drink your tap water unless it was highly filtered."

At that they both looked at the ceiling of the dining room where the pool water was reflecting by the light of the full moon.

"Highly filtered," Ernestine whispered.

They were both quiet for a minute till finally Ernestine said, "What about the rain water? In the rain barrels?"

"I can test it. I'll take some to work tomorrow."

"Don't tell anyone," she told him as she followed him out to the backyard with a clean mason jar in her hands.

"I won't."

**

CHAPTER SIX

"State of emergency has been declared in California. Severe water restrictions are being enforced throughout the entire state," Ernestine heard as she watched the national news. The rest of the country and her own state weren't faring so well either she found out when the commercial break was over.

"These southern counties are under a boil order until further notice," the news anchor said without once looking at the camera as he read a long list that included the southern half of Illinois.

"Meanwhile waters are testing for high levels of flammable chemicals in Kentucky, Tennessee and Missouri. Residents of southern Illinois fear this is the reason for the boil order in the lower half of their state."

"That wouldn't get rid of flammable chemicals," Ernestine muttered at the tv.

"Scientists came together in DC to debate where the chemicals came from while the GOP pats itself on the back as water levels nationwide drop to the lowest levels in twenty years, proving to conservatives that climate change and global warming were all false worries. As reservoirs completely empty out, states are looking at neighboring waters in hope that help can be found there but no one has any water to spare."

Ernestine sipped milk from an old earthenware mug while she watched helicopter footage of miles and miles of sparse dry scrublands of California, Nevada, Utah, Arizona and then jumping to the Midwest to show jumpy footage from Kansas, and then Arkansas as the news showed the draught was nationwide.

"Tom Thompson of Thompson Springs held his own press conference in Palo Alto to assure everyone that there was enough Thompson water for everyone.

"Water is not a right. Water is a privilege of the first world and Thompson Springs will always have enough high quality water for Americans at a fair price everyone can afford. At Thompson Springs we always knew water was the most important resource in this great land and we've always taken care to keep your water clean, because we care about our customers."

"Sure, buddy," Ernestine grumbled at the blonde man on tv wearing sunglasses as he drank from a tall glass covered in moisture beads before addressing a menagerie of microphones.

She never took her eyes off the tv even as the phone rang and her hand crawled to the receiver without her eyes looking at it.

"Water jumped to $5 a gallon today, Ernestine, and gas $6."

"I didn't go buy water today," Ernestine confessed to her and chewed her nails and muted the tv.

"What were you doing?" her mother asked nearly in a panic.

"Testing water," Ernestine told her quietly.

Her mom didn't answer at all which meant Ernestine was supposed to tell her everything.

"My pool water tested the best. It was basically drinkable. The rain barrels had a couple of harmless microorganisms, plant things. The bottled water was fine. Maybe trace amounts of metals. But the tap water was bad. Not as bad as what we thought at first, and not as bad as they're saying on the news. But then we filtered it with a Brita and it was ok. We filtered some more with a fish filter pump to see what it'd do and it was ok."

"California and Nevada are completely dry."

"Yeah, I saw,"

"The roads are choked with Army, did you see that?"

"NO! Where'd you see that?"

"On the board. Someone shot footage with their drone. You haven't been on the boards in ages."

"I have too."

"Ernestine, the internet will never go down and the boards on Amazon will never attract attention. Get a hold of me on there. If you ever lose touch with me."

"What are you talking about?"

"I think they're going to relocate people."

"Why?"

"I've counted over one hundred school buses the past three days. Empty ones. All headed toward California. They're going to relocate people."

"Why though?"

"To control them."

Ernestine was speechless.

**

Ernestine spent the next three days driving to every superstore within a hundred mile radius and still the Prius was not full of water. The back hatch was barely full. The stores were about empty except the fill your own and she didn't trust those and only got three of them. She would ask Pete to test some before she'd buy more of it.

When she pulled up in her drive she was shocked to see her neighbor Robert on her porch. He was pressing her doorbell and leaning into it as if his body weight would make it louder.

Once again he didn't hear her silent car roll up the drive and he started and spun around fast on her porch as she opened her door.

"There you are," he growled and held a long envelope in his hand. "This is yours," he said and held it out to her. "It came to me by accident."

When she took it, she realized it was already opened.

"I never took you for the type," Robert said from where he still stood on her porch. He crossed his thick arms over his chest and stared at her as if waiting for her to open the mail.

"What type?"

"The gun type," he said and smirked. "Driving a Prius and all and working at the university."

"I don't work there anymore," she said flatly.

Ernestine pulled out the letter and found a card identical to her drivers license. It was her firearm ID card.

"What kind of gun are you getting?"

"I don't know yet."

"For personal protection, right?"

"Just to have," she said and began to unlock the door.

"For when it all goes to shit," Robert said as he stepped off her porch and then he made her jump by barking out a big laugh. "Because it is," he told her as he began to cross her drive back to his own house.

"It is what?" she called to him as she stood in her door.

"Going to shit."

Just then a helicopter flew over, bright yellow and blue with a big number thirteen on the side. She wondered if Brock Andrews or bubbled-headed Carol were in the chopper and then she put her new gun ID in her wallet.

**

"The lab's closed."

It was Pete and he was talking to her over the fence that night as she sat on her back porch and smoked her pipe as she waited for the frozen pizza to cook.

"What?" she asked as she inhaled and tried to hide the pipe and its pungent fumes in the cup of her hands. But Pete was gone. Then she heard the rusty spring on the gate and Pete was there on her porch in the dark.

"Lab's closed. Kids are being sent home."

"That wasn't on the news," Ernestine coughed out a ridiculously long plume of smoke and waved it away from where it had gone right toward Pete's face. But he didn't notice and instead he sat with his elbows on his knees and his face hidden in his hands. Ernestine felt buzzed and slightly amused. She knew it wasn't the right time for that but couldn't help it and couldn't stop staring at the curly wiry hair coming out of Pete's ears. She shook her head to try to sober up. This was her second time she'd filled the pipe tonight. She'd been too wired thinking about getting a gun and too worried about Robert opening her mail, Robert knowing she was going to get a gun. The Jack sometimes made her more wired so she had gone out back to smoke and was just getting calmed down with her second pipe full when Pete showed up. And now she realized she wasn't getting calmed down; now she was completely stoned.

"Are they closing the university?" she finally asked him.

"Yes, I wonder when it'll be on the news."

"You know what else wasn't on the news?" she asked him.

"What?"

"Come inside," she said, her voice slow and her welcoming hand gesture for Pete to follow her even slower. "I'll show you."

"Wow, holy cow, it's hot in here," was all Pete could say as he pushed his glasses back up his nose. The house was hot and he was sweating.

"Air quit working," Ernestine said and led him to her desk.

"Wow," he said again a couple of minutes later.

He was sitting at the desk looking at the screen of Ernestine's computer. She had found her mother and her mother's friends on the boards at Amazon and there were several videos posted, taken today from drones in Utah, California and Nevada. Army trucks full of soldiers and equipment clogged the desert roadways for miles and miles. The sun was very bright and the land looked cracked and blasted by heat. Men were running around with clipboards and machine guns with heavy gear strapped to their bodies. There were checkpoints and road blocks all over the desert and all the videos were jerky and very short.

The boards were choked with speculation and pure panic fueled on by the reports that drones were being shot down. People were now buying up drones as fast as .22 caliber bullets. Eyes and communication, everyone kept repeating. New posts were popping up right before their eyes. The paranoia was deep.

"Eyes and communication," Ernestine whispered.

"They're closing all of Utah and Southern California. They're closing all of Southern Nevada. No one in. No one out. What does that mean?" Pete asked her from where he still sat in her office chair.

"I don't know."

"Isn't your mom down there? You should go get her."

"I don't think anyone can get in."

"Or out," Pete said, looking back at the screen. "Just like at the university."

"We won't be able to test any more water," Ernestine said and looked at him.

"We won't be able to buy any more water if the stores are all empty."

"Good thing I have my own," Ernestine said and then gulped as Pete looked at her. She wanted to say, I'll share with you. But she didn't.

That night after Pete went home, Ernestine watched the eleven o'clock news and waited for her mom to call again as report after report came in of riots in Chicago, San Francisco, Los Angeles, and Orlando. Ernestine couldn't tell if the people in the big cities were fighting to get out of them or fighting to stay in. In poorer neighborhoods locals were burning and looting and smashing everything in sight. Ernestine scooted closer to the tv to see if they were carrying water out of the stores they were looting. But it looked like booze and cigarettes. She shook her head.

"Good choices though," Ernestine agreed as she went to the front window to look out at her own dark street.

That night Ernestine stayed up till after 2 in the morning watching CNN and live coverage around the nation as chaos broke out. Tom Thompson was interviewed in his home which was fortified with security guards wearing Kevlar.

"The government has failed us," he said to the microphone held out to him as he stood on his back patio, beyond his pool, near a stone wall looking down on a valley of Southern California.

From this distance the traffic and homes looked like twinkly lights. But Ernestine knew from earlier reports that all of Southern California was completely falling apart. People of all races and social standings were looting and burning and a few were trying to flee the state. Just a few. She wondered if they would be able to get out, get into Nevada or if the Army would stop them.

"How has the government failed us?" the reporter shoved her microphone closer to Thompson who was still staring out at the city.

"They never got around to taking everyone's guns," he said without looking at her.

"Is this a gun problem?" she asked him.

"No, but it will be. When the people get thirsty enough."

"Back to you in the studio," she said as Thompson walked away from her, setting his full glass of water on the stone wall as he went.

"What seems to have started all of these riots, Blake?" the CNN Studio reporter asked her counterpart.

"Well Sharon, it was a powder keg. But what lit the match was," the anchorman said as the screen faded to prerecorded footage of men in suits with clipboards exiting black SUVs in droves and heading into an old art deco building with "City Municipal Works" carved on a sign on the front of it. "What lit the keg, Sharon, was the coordinated visits throughout the nation's largest municipalities by the EPA for surprise water tests, and then the coordinated shutting off of the cities' entire water supplies."

Ernestine watched and ticked off on her fingers the number of cities whose water was completely shut off as they showed Chicago, St. Louis, New York, Detroit, Kansas City, Denver, Las Vegas, Los Angeles, San Francisco, and San Diego.

"These weren't the only cities who had their water abruptly and completely shut off today. Reports of chaos from all over the nation are being reported and too numerous and too violent to show them all, Sharon."

"This was not received by the citizens well, I take it, Blake?"

"Not at all, Sharon. Martial Law has been declared around the nation as the Reserves are called in."

Ernestine rushed to her own kitchen to see if the water was shut off and heaved a sigh of relief as the water gushed out of the faucet at full force into the sink. She filled every pan she owned and began boling them on the stove.

**

CHAPTER SEVEN
TWO MONTHS LATER

Ernestine heard the mail slot flip flop in the front room but didn't hear any mail drop. Mail hadn't been delivered in two months but Ernestine still always listened for the mail drop and could hear the difference between a pile of bills or a bunch of sales papers or catalogues. She hated the sliding sound of bills falling through the slot. She didn't really like the other mail much either except for the catalogues that sold the hodgepodge of blankets and sun catchers and neat things that all had suns and moons on them. Today, it sounded like nothing fell through the slot and when she peeked her head around the corner of the dining room to look at the front door she felt sickened as she saw one small postcard on the hardwood floor.

WE'RE COMING TO YOUR NEIGHBORHOOD SOON! It said in huge happy letters on top of a sandy beach photo. Ernestine hesitated before turning it over. What could the water company possibly want now? There had been a boil order for two months in all of Illinois. There had been riots sporadically every other night or so in Chicago for seventy days. There had been bloody battles fought for water up north in the Windy City. The Army Reserves were called in and Martial Law declared and civil unrest was erupting nonstop.

Ernestine was glad that she lived far down state and away from all that. There had been no rain for nearly four months and the temperatures had been in the 90's all through May and creeping higher and higher every day in June. It was almost the Fourth of July and the temps were edging closer to 100 every day. Ernestine was certain something bad was going to happen on that day. She just felt it. She was so upset about its impending arrival that she had been on the pot all day that afternoon. 100 degrees was the kind of weather that would push everyone over the edge.

"115 down here," she could hear her mom saying in her head.

At least her rain barrels were dried up. There was just a thin layer of dry algae at the bottom of them and Pete had told her to keep that in there for when she collected rain in them again. He said it was healthy to have that growing in there. She was glad they were dry as the police cars prowled the streets day and night. She was terrified of being arrested for collecting rain water.

Ernestine flipped the postcard over in her dry fingers, unable to wait anymore to see what they wanted.

"We'll be in your neighborhood July 10-15 to register you for recovery services and relocation! Your well-being means alot to Illinois Water and we value your patronage and look forward to serving you in the future!"

For a while all she could think was, a lot is two words, you idiots. And that thought alone circled around and around in a dizzying circle in her mind till she squeezed her eyes shut.

The day had finally come, and as Robert had once said to her, it had all gone to shit.

Relocation.

That was all Ernestine could think. Relocation.

A crushing weight of dread and despair sat itself on her chest as she looked at the postcard and for five whole minutes she couldn't move. She couldn't even form one idea. All she could do was stand there, staring at the postcard until it began to blur in front of her eyes because she was crying too hard. A beach photo on the postcard for relocating people in the middle of the country. That was supposed to make people happy, she supposed.

But just last week in the news a little two year old boy had been at the beach in San Diego collecting shells with his family in three inches of water and his parents took their eye off him for two seconds and he was gone. Just completely gone. Sucked out by the tide. And they had to go home to South Dakota without him. Better that, she guessed, than being eating alive by amoeba from the inside out.

But how was the beach a happy place, when the news was reporting daily on people dying from brain eating amoebas and losing limbs and life from flesh eating bacteria they had been infested with from swimming at a beach? The news had just reported last night how Florida's waters were completely gummed up with an orange slimy bacterial algae that had surrounded the peninsula on all sides. The beaches were deadly now. Ernestine wailed in her head as she cried harder.

"Mom," she blubbered into the phone, "what am I going to do?"

"I don't know, you can't stay there. You have to get out. Come down here to me."

"Just leave the house? Leave everything?"

"Leave it all. Pack your car and come down here. Right now today."

"Ok Mom I will. But don't you think, don't you think they'll relocate you too? You're in the driest part of the country."

"Nahh, they don't care about us out here in the desert. There ain't no water to even fight over."

"What will we do?" Ernestine gasped thinking about her and her mother living out in the desert without any water.

"We'll figure it out. We'll make it work."

Ernestine snorted against the back of her hand and wiped her eyes and promised her mom she'd call every time she stopped for gas, which wouldn't be that often. The Prius could get 53 miles to the gallon and it held 9 gallons in the tank. Doing math made Ernestine calm down. She loved crunching numbers. Miles and gallons and hours and such all ran together in her head like a children's educational cartoon sung to some banjo song.

She ran upstairs and got a suitcase from the spare bedroom and opened it on her bed.

"Underwear, cargo pants, shorts, sport bras and underwear and a hoodie. That should be enough."

She stuffed in her brush, her big comb, her deodorant, and her toothbrush and the new tube of Crest. And then she stuffed in an extra pair of running shoes and zipped it up.

"Ok," she said to herself and straightened up and tucked a few fly away fluffs that had escaped her braid back behind her ears. "Water and food for the road and maybe some extra water and food for Mom's."

She lugged the heavy suitcase down to the front door. The bright afternoon sun sliced through a gap in the curtains and divided the room in half. Months without rain. More than six months with hotter and hotter temperatures and stricter water conditions daily. Boil orders were never going to be lifted. People were falling ill, dying, rioting, and killing each other for water, lack of water, or because of infected water. It was a pretend fantasy that wouldn't end. As she flew down the basement steps she wondered if her own water stockpiling and worries had caused God to curse her with this reality that was crushing her will to move.

But no, she was moving. She was throwing of cans of chili and cans of fruit into grocery sacks. She was lugging cases of small water bottles up the stairs and she was carrying gallon jugs up four at a time.

It was a reverse trip to the store, she thought and giggled and she realized how close to losing her grip she was.

Ernestine shielded her eyes as she stepped out on the porch. She glanced left at Pete's and right to Robert's as if checking to see if it was safe to cross her yard and load her car. But the block was deserted in all directions. She could only hear the screech of a complaining Blue Jay.

Finally her car was loaded; the back seats were folded flush down and the back was full of food and water and first aid things and her suitcase and a sleeping bag too. She had a road atlas and four state maps on the passenger seat along with two phone chargers, her laptop and two bottles of water in the center drink cup holder.

She was all ready. She consulted her map of Illinois and her atlas one last time. She would take 70 west the entire way. She didn't even need to plug it into the GPS, it was that simple; 70 all the way to Moab UT. She didn't want to put her mom's address in the GPS; she didn't want any digital record of where she was going.

She gave one last look up at her house and slid the gear into reverse and rolled backwards out of the drive.

"Goodbye house," she said and drove away. She was sad for a moment but then she thought only of her mother and she smiled as she drove down the road.

**

CHAPTER EIGHT

"What do you mean I can't leave the state?"

Ernestine got as far as the entrance to the Shawnee National Forest and was stopped in a line of trucks, cars, and an overwhelming number of RVs. She rolled down her window and even unbuckled and stuck her head out to see what was happening. That was when she saw the tall state trooper in the crisp brown slacks walking down the road between all the cars.

"Sir? Sir?" she called to him. "What's happening up there sir? An accident?"

"County lines are all closed and state lines are all closed too. No one in, no one out. All civilians are required to remain in place till the registration. No one can leave the state."

"What do you mean I can't leave the state? What's happening?" she cried.

"They're turning everyone around, ma'am."

"But what's happening?" she demanded in almost a wail.

"It's a mess, ma'am."

Polite to the end, he tipped his hat to her and stepped into the oncoming lane and stopped the traffic and waved at her and helped her pull out of line and do a u-turn.

Ernestine was in tears as she unloaded her car.

**

Ernestine's mom told her again and again that it'd be ok. That the state just wanted to do a head count down there in the southern boonies to see who all was living there so they could take better care of them during this crisis.

Ernestine disagreed but she was quiet about it. Her mom was trying to make her feel better, she knew that, but maybe her mom was trying to make herself feel better too.

"I'll be fine, Ernestine. Don't worry about me. There's a pump and a well at the KOA. No one goes there and hasn't in twenty years. Or maybe even more. So I have water and I don't eat much and Foxy's is still there and that's where I get all my food. Cheer up Ernestine. And get on the boards. I did something today that'll make you laugh."

Ernestine got on her laptop and found her mother on the Amazon boards where she'd reviewed a metal garbage can. The review was just a cover for what she really wanted people to see. She'd posted a picture of herself in a flowery swim cap and swimsuit huddled down in the garbage can full of water.

"Made my own little pool today" was typed out below her picture.

Ernestine saw a pump with a long handle right next to her mom. She could see that her mom had attached a bright green hose to the spigot.

"Only way to keep cool in this here hot desert," her mom had posted. Her face was shiny with the heat and darker than she'd ever been.

"Haha!" Ernestine broke out laughing on the phone to her mom.

"You get down here and you can get your own pool right next to mine," her mom said cheerfully. "Bring your bike!" she added.

Ernestine was silent.

"Don't worry, honey. Get registered then things will open up and you'll come down here."

"Ok, Mom."

And that's what she tried to do the next day. The registration was like nothing she'd ever seen. First off she couldn't drive to it. She tried but once again the roads were all clogged and state cops and local cops and army reserves were everywhere. She tried to drive downtown where the registration was taking place at the county building but only got a couple of blocks from it and had had to turn around and come home.

"You can't drive down there," Pete called to her from his drive.

But before she could respond to him, her other neighbor Robert called out, "It's a clusterfuck! How do they expect us to comply to their bullcrap if we can't even go anywhere in our cars?" His face was beet red and the tendons stood out in his neck.

"Were you actually gonna do it?" she asked him surprised.

"I was gonna sign up on the remainder lists," he growled.

"What's that?" Pete asked as he now stood in her yard.

"People that don't want any government help can claim remainder status. They're gonna scoop up all the wussies who can't take care of themselves and relocate them to some government housing, somewhere. They ain't said where but I've heard," he said and came closer to them and spoke in a hushed voice, "I've heard they're taking folks down to Kansas."

"Kansas?" Pete honked out in a laugh with his voice cracking. "Kansas," he said quieter after a glare from Robert who towered over him by six inches. "Why would they take us to Kansas?"

"Leavenworth," was all Robert whispered. And then he added, "They're not taking me."

"Me either," Ernestine breathed out. She looked at Pete and saw that his eyes were huge and his face had blanched. White people could turn all sorts of shades of white, she thought.

"You signing up for the remainders?" Robert asked and now seemed interested in her.

"If I have to sign anything at all. How would they know if we didn't sign up at all?"

"Oh, I think they'd know," Pete said pushing his glasses up his nose.

"Oh, they'd know all right," Robert agreed.

"I'm going to walk down there, want to go with me?" Pete asked.

"No thanks," Ernestine and Robert said at the same time.

"Too hot right now," Ernestine said and wiped her brow and looked up at the sun. Not one single cloud in the sky.

"Good day for a swim," Robert growled and strode off to his front door, his freckled legs flexing as he went.

Ernestine gulped and went in the house where the air conditioner was working hard again but didn't seem to be making a difference. She plopped down in her big chair and turned on the 24 hour news station.

California seemed to be entirely on fire; buildings, homes on hills, homes in valleys, the very mountains themselves. Traffic zoomed by in front of the camera on the freeway and Ernestine wondered how they didn't all crash into each other.

"All of Los Angeles is surrounded by an inferno, Bill," a woman's voice said over the footage of cars zooming down a freeway at what must have been 80 miles per hour.

Ernestine scooted up onto the edge of her chair to get a closer look at the tv. Now there was a map with large red flame shaped symbols placed around it as the feed went back to the studio.

"As you can see here, here and here," the female reporter said and pointed her long red nail at the red flame symbols, "the fires completely surround the metro area. And these fires, Bill, each cover upwards of 500 yards."

"That's 5 football fields, Wanda!"

"That's right Bill."

"That's a lot of yardage!"

"That's why I stated it that way Bill, I know you can't hardly wait for football season to pick back up."

"That's right, Wanda."

And on they joked as they showed footage around Los Angeles of fires raging through the wealthiest neighborhoods and even raging downtown through the financial district.

Mayhem seemed to be breaking out across the nation. Riots in Chicago. Poor neighborhoods on fire. Thousands of people in the streets. Lake Shore Drive was completely shut down with cops, ambulances, fire trucks, and people. The tollways were choked with military. Humvees and armored vehicles drove up and down all major tollways. Chicago was a city of people from every nation and it looked like a mini world war with the nationalities all forming their own little armies within the neighborhoods of the city. The suburbs were on lockdown. No one in, no one out. El trains had been pushed over on their sides and black smoke boiled out of the broken windows.

Worse things than riots were happening all over the rest of the nation. Hundreds of people were dying in Ohio, Arkansas, Minnesota, North Carolina and West Virginia the news reporter said from "Naegleria Fowleri". She said it three times, exaggerating her red lips around the name.

"Brain eating bacteria, Bob," she stated now in a grave tone.

"Wow, Wanda, I can't tell which one sounds more horrific."

"Horrific indeed, Bob. Six hundred and four people have been reported as having been infected by it and have died from it in the past two days."

"I thought this was the one you got from swimming in waters and it went up your nose, Wanda. Have people been hitting the old swimming holes harder because of the heatwave?"

"That's right Bob except for one. Prailine Newberry of Mobile, Alabama hasn't been swimming in a lake in over seventy years."

"That's a long time," Bob said thoughtfully.

"That's right. She was 93 and she contracted the brain eating amoeba without leaving her home. The CDC was reluctant to say on record but this is the first case of someone contracting the amoeba from their own tap water. Now whether she came in contact from drinking it or say something as innocent as washing her face, we don't know yet. An autopsy is scheduled and we'll report back on that in a few days. Meanwhile the EPA is testing her water and her house has been sealed as a crime scene. The CDC did say the other six hundred and three deaths from all over the nation are all confirmed that the victims were all recently swimming in fresh water."

"Not that fresh of water, Wanda."

"Not at all, Bob. Takes away the magic from the old nostalgic watering hole."

"I think I'll stick to my own pool in my backyard."

"I've heard about your pool, it's really something is what they say."

"It is Wanda. I'll have to have your family over."

Ernestine harrumphed and figured it'd be a cold day in hell when Wanda and her black family was welcomed to Bob's neighborhood.

"We'd love that. Now let's go to Rasheeda Bond who has the latest video about the riots now taking place in the south."

Video footage of the protests in the south showed all the Bible thumpers had come together; the white Evangelicals, the snake handlers, and the Black Baptists, the overweight white Baptists, and even the Catholics, all with huge neon signs proclaiming the end, blaming the gays, blaming the atheists, blaming the aliens even, as they marched down the streets. They were surrounded by great swirling brawls of people. The gun carrying camo wearing survivalists were shouting at a contingency of people wearing rainbow shirts and carrying rainbow signs and posters of hand painted Earths and flowers. The streets were roiling with human anger and cries of the end of the world from Texas on through Oklahoma, Louisiana, Mississippi, Alabama, Georgia, Florida, the Carolinas and on up to Kentucky, Missouri and getting real close to Southern IL to where Ernestine lived. How had things gotten to this this fast? Ernestine asked herself as the news showed helicopters bringing in huge pallets of water to the outstretched arms of the unwashed masses.

Ernestine watched the news for hours till she made herself sick to her stomach and then she read the news on her phone as she sat on the toilet. Finally she turned if off and just dropped her phone on the bathroom rug. She sat for another fifteen minutes with her head hanging almost to her knees and emptied herself out.

She worried for a moment that she had her own amoeba. But not in her head.

Finally after she was done, she went into the front room, clicked off the tv and collapsed on the couch. A puff of old cigarette smoke and musk gently poofed out of the cushions, reminiscent of her ex-husband who had spent many hours on the couch, drinking, smoking, cussing at the news. But the afternoon was warm and the roar of the air conditioner as it tried to make a dent in the heat, lulled her to sleep. The last thought in her head was, I should get a new couch, before her eyes fluttered shut and she fell asleep.

**

Flip-flop.

The sound of the mail slot woke her with a jolt to the heart. Just the flip-flop and no sound of mail hitting the floor. Then she heard a crinkle and the sharp whisper of a postcard drifting close to the wood floor before landing on it.

WE ARE IN YOUR NEIHBORHOOD TODAY! HAVE YOU REGISTERED YET? DON'T FORGET!

That was all it said. Still the happy photo of the sunny beach and the bright plastic toys.

Don't forget.

Ernestine rubbed her eye that she had slept on smooshed against the arm of the couch without a pillow and threw the postcard in the small garbage can on her way to the bathroom. She pulled her hair out of her braids, combed through it all and braided it up again, tighter.

She drank two glasses of water poured from a gallon jug and then looked at the clock. 4:30. She startled herself with the hasty idea of why didn't she just walk downtown right now and register and get it done? Why didn't she? She asked herself again. She rubbed her eyes and slipped on her sport sandals and grabbed her purse, locked up the house and started out.

She'd nearly gotten to the corner when Robert fell in step beside her.

"Registering?" he asked.

She looked over at him and saw he was dressed almost identical to her. She had cut a pair of camouflaged cargo pants off at the knees to make shorts and she had them on with an old black t-shirt. Robert also had on camouflaged pants cut off at the knee and made into shorts and an old black t-shirt too. But he had on steel toed work boots instead of sandals. They clomped with every heavy step he took.

"I guess we're dressed for it"

"For the registration?" she asked.

"They'll know we're gun nuts just by looking at us."

"I'm not," she said but was now worried. She didn't want to seem like a gun nut to the people at this registration. She wanted to seem harmless. She was harmless. She just wanted to be left alone.

Robert raised his eyebrows and smirked at her. "You are too," he said.

"I don't even own a gun."

"You better buy one before it's too late. While they'll still let you. While there's still some left to buy. With the entire world going to shit you can bet people are buying up guns and ammo like mad."

Ernestine silently agreed and made a note to herself to stop at the bank and withdraw the money while she was downtown. For some reason she thought she'd leave less of a trail if she paid cash.

They were silent as they walked together downtown. She was anxious to see how crowded it was. She was worried it was going to be a scene like Chicago with rioting but all seemed quiet in the neighborhood. When they mounted the hill leading into the square they were both audibly disappointed. There were only about thirty people milled about waiting in front of five long folding tables. There were only a few police and no military at all now. It looked almost like a grass roots rally for some far-fetched politician who would never garner enough votes to do anything.

When Ernestine and Robert got closer to the tables they saw they were divided up by last name and as Ernestine went to the A-F table Robert stepped away to the N-R table. By the time her turn came, there was no one else at her table but the three men manning it.

"Hello," she said with a lump in her throat. She felt dumb. She felt like she should know why she was there, what she was expected to do.

It went the same as voting on election day; name, address, phone number, and then they asked, "Do you opt for State Assistance or do you wish to remain?"

"Do I have a choice?"

"Of course you do," the man on the left end of the table said to her, and smiled at her with his capped teeth. He looked like a tanned golf player except his clothes were a little ragged and rumpled. "But if you choose remainder status, you should know there will be no water, or utilities, and no police or protection. This area will be evacuated." And at this he dropped his chin just a fraction and his smile completely disappeared. His eyes were bloodshot and close together and she didn't like him at all and signed her name on the list without leaning too close to him.

"When is this happening?"

"We will let you know," was all he said.

Ernestine didn't like that at all. She liked to know when things were happening; especially her neighborhood being shut down, evacuated, utilities turned off. She needed to know that. She thought hard for a few seconds before getting the nerve to ask her next question.

"Will we be allowed to leave the state?"

The man with the capped teeth and bloodshot eyes stared at her hard before smiling and saying, "Of course you will. But why would you want to? Where would you go? The state is providing free relocation for everyone to the assistance recovery area. No personal vehicles are allowed."

Ernestine's heart trip-hammered and she just wanted to go home. She wanted to take back her registration as a remainder. She wanted to rip the ream of papers out of this man's hands and get rid of all record of her. She glanced over to see if Robert was still registering and didn't see him anywhere and for a moment she had a bit of vertigo and felt dizzy and only when she felt a slight breeze on her damp neck, did she feel better.

"Ma'am?" Another man at the table was asking her something.

"Am I done here?" she asked them.

"Yes ma'am. Here," he was holding something out to her. It looked like a small green and white sticker about 6x6 inches in size. "Put this in your front door ma'am so the patrols will know you're a remainder." He smiled up at her from where he sat as if he'd just given her something wonderful.

She took the sticker without looking at it and started to step away from the table. But then she saw a stack of red stickers on the end of the table. They said, "Relocated" on them.

"Oomp!" she cried out as she crashed into the corner of the table with her hip and landed with her body on top of the stack of red stickers. But she did it too hard and she crashed head over into the man with the capped teeth, knocking him over backwards in his chair.

"Ooof!" she cried as she rolled off him and ground her elbow into the pavement.

Her goal had been to grab a stack of the red stickers, but she missed.

"Let me help you up."

Suddenly Robert was there and he was pulling her up by her arm, being careful to not touch her elbow, which now felt like it was on fire.

**

"Is this what you were going for?" Robert finally broke the silence when they were nearly home.

He pulled a stack of only mildly bent red square stickers from his side cargo pocket. "What'd you want these for?" he asked her as she took them.

"I don't know," Ernestine answered slowly, "I just know I'm not putting that other sticker in my window."

"We're both remainders," Robert said as they both stopped on the sidewalk in front of their drives.

Without talking they both looked over at Pete's quiet little cape cod. They could see he had his red square sticker up in the long slender window next to his front door.

"Can I have one of those?" Robert asked, and nodded toward the red stickers in her hand.

She gave him one without speaking.

"You better get inside and clean up that wound," was all he said and he left her standing there as he went in his house.

"I forgot to go to the ATM," she said to no one and got in her car and drove back to the now empty and deserted downtown. But the ATM would only let her withdraw $200; not nearly enough for her. So she went back home frustrated but determined to come back.

The next morning found her at the doors of the bank at 8AM but the bank didn't want to let her withdraw $1000, which she thought was the amount she'd need for a new gun, ammo, a case, and money left over for water and gas and whatever else. The bank wanted to know why she wanted it.

"I need it. To buy things."

"Yes, but what?"

Ernestine took one step back from the counter and frowned, confused. She didn't owe the bank an explanation.

"This is my money, is it not?" she asked as she stepped back closer to the counter and gripped it with her fingers.

"Yes," the teller replied, and he himself now stepped back a pace from her.

"I don't answer to you," she said to him quietly. "Do I?"

"No, ma'am. And there's no need to take a tone."

"I'm not taking a tone. You'll know when I take a tone. I want to close my accounts," she said and her voice wavered.

"There's no need to get sassy."

"I want to close my accounts. Now."

"Are you certain there's money in there?"

"Would you even ask me this if I were white?"

"Ma'am, I'm going to need,"

"My account, my ID, I want my money," Ernestine said and slid her ID cards across the counter.

"I see," he said and cleared his throat several times. "Ok," he said and his fingers began to tap lightly on the keyboard several strokes and then he paused, cleared his throat a few times and kept typing. Finally he said, "One moment," and stepped away and disappeared through a door behind the counter.

Ernestine waited and waited shifting from foot to foot. People were staring at her. Workers and customers both paused in their business and looked at her.

"I only want $50," a man next to her told his teller and then looked at Ernestine with a nasty curl to his lips.

She stood there for eight whole minutes; she timed it on the clock, then finally the teller returned with a woman in a red pantsuit. She had blonde hair cut in a severe, choppy, asymmetrical style that was shorter and spikier in the back and straight and stiff in the front.

"How may I help you today?" she asked crisply as if she didn't already know what Ernestine wanted.

"I want to close my accounts."

"Do you have an appointment with someone in checking?" She looked Ernestine up and down as she asked her.

"No," Ernestine said and felt like she were stuck in between crying and screaming.

"Well you'll need an appointment with someone in checking. The front desk will be happy to help you schedule one," Red Pantsuit said to her and smiled again.

One of her eye teeth had a yellow coffee stain and Ernestine stared hard at it.

"I don't want an appointment. I just want to make a withdrawal. I want to withdraw MY money." Ernestine paused and waited for Red Pantsuit or the teller to dispute this and when they were silent she asked, "What is my exact balance?"

The male teller scooted in front of the woman and began his light tapping on the keyboard again while he eyed Ernestine's account ID card again. He licked his lips several times and said, "Nine thousand one hundred fifty-six dollars and thirteen cents in savings and," and here he tapped some more. "Two thousand three hundred and twenty nine dollars and seventy-five cents in checking."

"Ma'am," Red Pantsuit pushed in front of the teller and said to Ernestine, "Ma'am you cannot close your account today."

"I'm not."

Ernestine did some quick calculations in her head and filled out two new withdrawal slips.

"Nine thousand from savings and two thousand from checking," she said and slid the slips to the teller.

"Whatever do you want with?" he started to ask and saw the look on her face and began his light tapping again. "You should probably leave some in checking to cover any e-payments," he said without looking at her.

"E-payments? Who's gonna be around to take e-payments?" Ernestine asked a little too loud.

"Ma'am. We're going to have to ask you to leave," Red Pantsuit lady bumped the teller out of the way as he counted the money.

"Hundreds, just give me hundreds," Ernestine told him around Red Pantsuit.

"Ma'am," she said with an edge in her voice.

"I am leaving as soon as I get my money."

The teller counted faster and faster. He made two piles. He counted it again.

"Kevin, that won't be necessary. She's leaving. She's not getting her money today."

Red Pantsuit's eyes were bulging out of her head and the skin around her mouth was turning white.

"But I've already done it on the computer, Deedra."

"Put it back!"

Now Deedra was trying to shove the teller completely away from the window as he stood there with two thick stacks of cash in his hands.

"But Deedra, it's already done," he whined to her. "I can't have this discreprency on my drawer!" he said angrily. Clearly she was his supervisor but maybe not so high up that she couldn't keep him from getting in trouble about a mistake with his drawer.

"Kevin, Deedra?"

Now they were joined by a small man in a suit with white hair and a white trim mustache.

"Is there a problem?"

"I've already taken her money out on the computer Mr. Shrimpton, I have to give it to her, policy says, but Deedra is telling me not to."

"Is there a reason to not give our customer her withdrawal?" Mr. Shrimpton asked, and his eyes bulged as he looked at the two stacks of bills Kevin the teller held.

"No sir, I just, no sir," Deedra sighed and stepped aside.

"No, you were just being racist," Ernestine hissed at her.

Ernestine, Mr. Shrimpton, and Deedra all watched as Kevin counted the two stacks of money one last time. Ernestine counted it with him, in her head, so when he gave it to her in two big envelopes, she didn't feel she needed to count it again. She dropped them in her big purse and left.

After that, she was too nervous to go gun shopping and just went home and hid her money in a cereal box in the basement behind all the water.

She hovered about the house cleaning and counting water and organizing her basement while she waited for the cover of darkness to go out back and smoke her pipe and try to calm down.

CHAPTER NINE

"Will you go with me to buy a gun?" Ernestine couldn't believe she was doing this. She was on Robert's porch right after lunch the next day asking him for help.

She'd made herself sick to her stomach after the bank fiasco and after thinking about buying a gun on her own. They would know she didn't know a whole lot about guns any more. She used to know a little. But it'd been almost ten years since she'd been around them. Since she'd been shooting. If the bank didn't want to let her take out her own money, how could she expect a gun shop to sell her a gun she knew nothing about?

Robert rubbed his eyes and then rubbed his shaved head and Ernestine realized she had woken him up.

"I'm sorry. This is a bad time," she mumbled and turned around to leave.

"No, no, I must have dozed off. They closed the plant."

Ernestine turned around when he didn't say anything else.

"They closed the plant and I guess I just fell asleep on the couch. Here," he said and opened the screen door.

Ernestine hesitated and then went in to Robert's small front room. It was dark and smelled like last night's cooking. His couch was camouflaged and oversized. There was a painting of two ducks in flight on the wall and a big tv on the other.

"If you don't have time, I can go by myself."

"No, I can go. It'll be fun. Let me brew some coffee for the road."

Ernestine counted her money again while he was in the kitchen. She had $1000 in her purse.

"Let's go shopping!" Robert announced with a smile when he came back to the front room, and raised his travel mug of coffee to her with a big smile.

But she didn't get to do much shopping. The gun store was packed and there was a one gun per customer limit. Ernestine feared a riot was going to break out. She would have never even went in without Robert. But he pushed their way through all the NRA hat wearing men to the counter. Ernestine blended in with them in her camo pants and t shirt, even though she was half their size and the only woman and the only black person.

"Let's just get you something simple and when you come back in three days and pick up, you can purchase something else."

"Ok," she agreed. She was completely out of her element and couldn't process anything she was seeing. She left the store with $360 less in her pocket and a receipt for a Smith and Wesson 38 special that she could pick up in three days.

"Bullets," she said flatly in the car. "I should have got bullets."

"Let's head to Tractor Supply. You can stock up there. They're cheaper there."

Tractor Supply was packed. Ernestine had to go back outside to find a cart. Robert came back out with her and found one too.

"How many boxes you want?" Robert asked her from where he stood in front of all the green and yellow cardboard boxes.

"All of them."

"Calm down, Calamity, there's a limit," Robert chuckled. "Five."

"Five then and as many boxes for the gun you think I'll order in three days."

Robert raised his eyebrows at her and then smiled and picked out five boxes of 9mm to go with the .38s.

"I need to get water," Ernestine stuttered as they made their way towards the registers.

"Good idea," Robert agreed.

Ernestine followed him as they pushed their carts through the chaotic and crowded store. They both filled their carts with jugs of water.

"It's a wonder more people," Robert started to say, but was cut off by a vibrating Hoom! sound as he put two more jugs in his cart.

A loud bang reverberated off the ceiling of the whole store and the lights hummed on brighter and then crackled, and then all of them snapped off.

People began to scream and yell and Ernestine grabbed the handle of her cart and squatted down instinctively behind it.

"Jesus!" Robert exclaimed and then emergency lights came on at intervals throughout the store, blinking and dim.

They were near the entrance by the snacks and the popcorn machine and nowhere near the exit or the registers. The sunlight outside the entrances was blinding to those inside the murky store.

"Stay here with the carts," he told her. "I'll go see what's happening."

Ernestine peeked around the cart from where she still squatted and watched him tromp off in the dark and shadowy store. People were crying and yelling and it sounded like an argument with many contributors was starting up by the registers; the direction Robert had gone.

She tried to wait but the sound of the voices growing louder and angrier was scaring her and she couldn't stay there. Slowly,

Ernestine pushed Robert's cart full of water and ammo and shotgun shells towards the front of the store as she pulled her cart behind her with her other hand. She was still trying to hunch down behind Robert's cart as she went. Her breathing sounded fast and quivery in her own ears and she felt as if she were going to pass out if she didn't get out of the dark soon. As she got closer to the entrance the voices got louder. The cashiers were telling people to be patient. People were abandoning their carts and pushing their way through the closed sliding glass doors. A group of men were arguing, clustered around one of the registers. She strained to see Robert's silhouette in the gloom of the emergency lights but she couldn't make him out as she pushed and pulled closer and closer to the doors.

She was just going to walk out with the carts. She didn't even question why she was stealing. She just needed to get out of the store and she needed to get out with her water and her ammo. And she was taking Robert's with her. He could meet her at the car. Eventually he'd come out, she said to herself. She was nearly at the entrance and the doors were already pushed open about a foot. She was picking up speed when suddenly a man yelled, "Everything's free! Screw it!" He yelled it so loud his voice cracked and it sounded painful in Ernestine's ears.

She turned to her right to look to see where the yelling man was. He was in the vicinity where Robert had gone. She heard yelling and saw a mass of people that way and then, POP! POP-pop-POP-pop! All in a row with small blue white flashes in the dark store followed by shrieking as the mass of men ran in all directions. Except some didn't run. Some fell where they stood in heavy humps right on the floor in a jumble.

And then one was running. He was running right at Ernestine. A tall lean man with a face that shone in the sunlight that came through the door. He was covered in sweat and his eyes were huge and his mouth was wide open as he ran past Ernestine. She couldn't tell if he was the shooter or if he was running away from the shooter.

And then he was followed by another man. A larger man. Robert.

"ROBERT!" Ernestine yelled because he didn't even recognize her as he ran at her.

"Let's get out of here!" he screamed.

She was already turned toward the doors and shoving Robert's cart out as she yanked at hers behind her.

"Here!" he yelled and took her cart and they both shoved through the door; first her and then him and they ran as fast as the carts could be pushed to her car.

**

"Mom!" Ernestine said to her mom on the phone. She called her as soon as she got home.

Robert had helped her carry all her water and ammo in from where they had dumped it all together in the hatch of her car. She had waved him goodbye and told him she needed to lay down after that. But she had called her mom right away. "Mom!" she said again into the phone.

"121 here Ernestine," her mother interrupted her. "I saw your news, 102 there but we still got you beat."

"No, Mom," was all Ernestine could say.

"What?" Her mom finally asked after waiting a whole minute for Ernestine to speak.

She finally got it out.

"We got shot at."

That was all she could say. She tried to say more but all her mouth would do was make gold fish motions of opening and closing.

"Shot at? Good lord! By the police?" her mom hollered into the phone.

“No. Some guy. Down at the Tractor Supply.”

“Were you with your ex?”

“No Mom.”

“Well that’s where he always hung out and someone shooting at him; that I could believe, and understand. But why were they shooting at you?”

“They weren’t shooting just at me. They just started shooting. The power went out at the Tractor Supply Store and everybody panicked.”

“You all right?”

“I’m okay.”

“What were you doing there?”

“Buying ammo.”

“You sure you weren’t there with Ed?”

“I’m sure.”

“Who were you there with?”

“My neighbor.”

“The peacenik?” she asked and laughed.

“No, the other one.”

“Jarhead?”

“Yes, that one.”

“When can you come down here? Get away from the crazies up there and get down here to the desert.”

"Few days. I pick up my new pistol in two days and am gonna order another. Then I'll head down. I'm all registered with the state as a remainder. But I'm leaving."

"If they'll let you. They're giving everyone the chance here to get picked up by a bus and taken to Salt Lake City or Lake Tahoe."

"Did you want to go?"

"No, hell no. It ain't no vacation like they're making it out to be. I've got water at the KOA. I got no neighbors for five miles in any directions. I feel safe here. Relocation," her mother muttered. "They just want to take your pension and social security," she grumbled and gave Ernestine a jolt of panic as she thought of something she had forgotten.

"Mom, I gotta go! I forgot to do something!"

"All right be careful. Avoid the stores. You got enough water and enough ammo."

"Ok Mom."

Ernestine checked her braids in the mirror and grabbed her purse and left the house. But the road into campus was blocked.

"But I need to get to HR," she told the traffic cop who was making all traffic turn away from campustown.

"University is closed ma'am."

"But why? I need to change my direct deposit right away."

"Direct deposit?" he asked and came closer to her window. "Ain't gonna be no more direct deposit for anyone," he said and laughed and then he came so close to her window that he poked his head inside the shady cool air of her car; his sweaty red face an inch from her own. "They're relocating everyone. No one is gonna have a paycheck to worry about. We need to worry about the fall of our country, don't' you see?"

Ernestine stared at him. She wanted to get away from him but he was still leaning in her car.

"Why is the university closed?" she asked.

"They're getting rid of everyone. There's no water to be had for survival in this whole country. Don't you watch the news?" he asked and stepped away from her car and blew his whistle and waved her to go on and follow the detour away from the school campus.

Her cellphone was ringing when she got on her porch.

"Were you able to get anywhere?"

"Who is this?"

"It's Pete. Can I come over?"

"I guess."

"Were you able to get anywhere?" he asked again once he came in.

Ernestine ignored him as she drank right from a gallon jug of water. It was 102 out today and her AC in her house had completely stopped working. She had her blinds and curtains all pulled downstairs to keep the sun out but it was very stuffy and still incredibly hot in the house.

"Good day for a swim," Pete said as he nodded toward her back door.

"It is," she agreed and for the first time ever she actually thought about getting in her pool and maybe she would later. Much later. After she picked up her pistol and after it got dark.

"Were you able to get anywhere in your car?" he asked again.

"No," she said and wondered if Pete had been watching her out of his window.

"Where'd you try to go?"

"The university," she said and took another cold swig from the jug.

"Why'd you want to go there?"

She looked over at him but couldn't see his eyes from the glare off his glasses.

"I just ask because I would like to go. I'd like to get my microscope and stuff from the lab. I don't think the water's as bad as they say."

"What are they saying?"

"That it's undrinkable."

"Here?"

"Here right here," he said pointed at her floor.

"Hmph. Even boiled?"

"Yes. I'd like to get my stuff from the lab. Test it myself."

"Why? You're leaving right? You checked relocate on your registration?"

"Not if I don't have to, I'm not going, not if it's a hoax," he said as his face turned red.

Ernestine didn't like how close he was getting to her. He was also getting near hysterical and it made her nervous. It reminded her of being at the Tractor Supply the night before.

"Who would listen to you?" she asked him against her better judgement.

"Everyone who has a brain. And if no one did, then I wouldn't care. I'd just stay. I'd change my registration to remainder."

"Why don't you do that now anyway? What were you thinking?"

"If the water's poison, I'd have to go. You have enough water for you, but you're crazy to remain behind. There will be no police. It'll be dangerous to remain here alone."

It'll be dangerous to go, she wanted to say but kept quiet.

"I've got to try to get in my old lab. I know the back service road behind the cemetery that butts up against the back of the engineering campus by the steam plant. I'm going tonight. I'm going to prove to everyone the water's not as bad as they say it is. I wish I could borrow your Prius. It's quiet," he said and turned back to her from where he stood at her door.

"No. Get out. No. You're not using my car to break into school. No," she said to him and shoved him out the door. She watched him to make sure he went back to his own home.

"What's professor nitwit up to?"

Robert was on her porch. A small part of Ernestine looked forward to the relocation just so she'd have more peace and quiet.

"Hey, I came to see if you wanted to get your pistol?" he asked before she shut the door.

They rode in Robert's truck to Tim's Gun Shop and found it locked. Tim was inside behind the counter and because he knew Robert he let them in and quickly locked the door back up and pulled the shade.

"'Fraid of being looted. Got everything and I mean everything in the safe. You gotta receipt?" he asked Ernestine.

"Yes," she said as she eyed the black tattoos zigzagging up his arms.

He took the receipt and looked at it with reading glasses he pulled out of the pocket of his t-shirt.

"Why don't you two sit in my office while I go find it in the safe?" he beckoned to them to come behind the counter.

"I don't feel safe having you in the store," he told them and made Ernestine nervous. "No bars on the windows; someone's gonna loot. I can feel it," he told them and rubbed his short blonde hair several times and looked back at them; his eyes pale behind the thick reading glasses. "The sooner they relocate everyone the safer I'll feel."

He took them to a back office and offered them two chairs and told them he'd be right back. He pulled a small yellow notebook from the top drawer of a metal desk and thumbed it open to a page with eight numbers on it and then left them. Ernestine was anxious while they waited but Robert seemed completely relaxed, even when Tim was gone ten long minutes.

"You hear further up on the north side is completely without power?" Robert asked her.

"No." Ernestine had not heard of that on the news.

"Cops are over there like crazy trying to keep them from rioting. The relocation has to be happening soon. Get those crazy fools out of here before they burn the city down," Robert said and winced when he saw her face when he said 'fools'.

"Is that why the power went out at the store?"

"City is shutting down. Northside are the lucky ones I guess and got shut off first."

"It's always the poor who get it worst first," Ernestine mused.

"Liberal," Robert smirked at her.

"Why wasn't it on the news?" Ernestine asked in a worried voice.

"No one cares about the poor anymore," Robert said. "When the world is going to shit, no one cares about the poor anymore. When times are good, the poor and disadvantaged and the lazy asses on welfare are all over the news. But when everyone is going to hell in a handbasket together, no one cares about the poor anymore. There are no poor anymore. No welfare either. All that's left is guns and food. And in our world, water."

Ernestine didn't know what to say to him after this little speech. The world was happening too fast for her to process lately. She didn't know where she stood but thought maybe he was right because right now all she was worried about was getting her gun and keeping her water.

"I tried to go over there this morning. I felt bad about us not paying for all that stuff," Robert said to her. Ernestine stared at him in disbelief and he went on and said, "No one in and no one out. They turned me right around."

Robert cracked his knuckles as he looked around Tim's little office and Ernestine just sat quiet and stared at the Confederate flag that hung behind the desk. Then Tim came back with Ernestine's pistol in a box and she looked away from the flag quickly.

She opened the box on her lap from where she sat on the folding chair. She couldn't stop looking at it.

"You know how to load it? Shoot it?" Robert asked.

"Yes," she answered still looking at the heavy little pistol.

"From Ed, your ex?" Tim asked as he sat down and lit up a cigarette. He had big black tattoos even on the insides of his arms and on the tops of his hands.

"Yes, from Ed," she answered and looked away from his arms and up at his face to see if she recognized him but she didn't.

"He's a gun nut. Her ex," Tim said to Robert as if he had to explain. "Total gun nut, he's staying I take it," Tim said to Ernestine.

"I have no idea," she admitted quietly and put the pistol back in the box. "I'd like a shoulder holster and ammo and another pistol," she declared and stood up.

"I got no other weapons to sell," Tim told her as he dropped the little yellow notebook on his desk and stubbed the cigarette out and started to leave the room. "But I got lots of .38's and no limit and several holsters to choose, but make it quick," he said and left the room.

"After you," Ernestine told Robert and gestured for him to go in front of her and then they followed Tim back out to the store.

"I'm not gonna be here in two days, so I can't sell you another weapon," Tim said as he stacked boxes of .38's on the counter.

"You got a whole safe back there," Ernestine countered as she took a step back from the counter.

"Yes. But I can't sell any because like I said, I ain't gonna be anywhere near this town in two days. I'm laying low."

"Where?" she asked and stepped back up to the gun counter.

"Ain't saying."

"Sell me one now. I got cash. Sell me one off the books. Who'll know?"

"How much cash," he asked and licked his lips.

"Depends on what you're selling."

"What'd you have in mind?"

"9mm."

"I could lose my license over this."

"You could lose everything if they loot this store."

"Safe can't be cracked. It'd still be there. No one can get that thing open."

Ernestine let her money talk because she didn't know what else to say. She pulled out her envelope full of hundreds and twenties and watched Tim's eyes widen.

"Something small for her," Robert finally spoke up.

"9mm," Ernestine said. "Something that holds a lot of rounds."

"Good idea," Robert agreed. "And a few mags."

"Be right back, don't touch nothin'," Tim told them and left.

Ernestine bought a Ruger SR9C for $1000 cash unregistered. She bought four magss for $400. Robert bellowed and yelled and looked as if he was going to go over the counter and grab Tim by the collar but Ernestine calmed him down.

"It's all right. Times are different now," she told him as she peeled the money away from the stack while Tim watched her closely; he rubbed his head again several times as she counted.

"You can say that again. Anything else you need?" Now he was ready to sell as many unregistered guns as he could.

"No, we're done." It was Robert who answered.

Tim held up his hands in a surrendering gesture towards Robert who was looking agitated.

"You should load up both and strap them on and get out before it gets dark."

Ernestine put the .38 in a shoulder holster and the 9mm on her hip and the mags in her purse.

"Here, take these," Tim said and he carried over a handful of speedloaders for the .38 and one for the 9mm and dumped them in her purse. "I'm throwing these in for free."

"You ain't," she said.

"She paid," Robert added and they left.

"I wonder where he's gonna keep all his guns? There in the vault?" Ernestine asked when they got home.

She felt bulky and heavy and strange with two loaded pistols strapped to her body. She wondered if she walked weird when she got out of Robert's truck.

"Not at his hidey house," Robert laughed. "It's smaller than his safe!"

"You know where he's going?"

"Everyone knows he's got a trailer deep in the Shawnee Forest. Been in his family for generations. Only residence in that whole park."

"That's odd."

"It is. Just like Tim."

That night Ernestine worked hard to memorize the eight digit number on the little torn off piece of notebook paper. But her mind was too nervous to commit it to memory so she covered the piece of paper in clear packing tape to make it water proof and she tucked it into her wallet.

She felt nervous and jumpy and she didn't know if it was from stealing the combination or if it was from buying two pistols, which she was still wearing. She kept looking at herself with them on. She turned from side to side to see them strapped on her under her clothing. She turned from side to side to see if they were detectable but finally decided that she was so ordinary looking and so small that no one would ever guess that she was carrying two loaded guns.

She strapped them on so they were visible outside her clothing and admired herself in the mirror. She looked tougher now and not so ordinary. They were a lot easier to unholster when they weren't concealed but she wouldn't be able to do that. Then she took them off. She put the .38 in her side table with one box of ammo. The fifteen other boxes were stored down in the basement. The 9mm she tucked loaded in a box of sani pads in her bathroom. That ammo and mags went down in the basement in the old coal chute that she could get to from behind the furnace or she could get to from outside on the driveway. If there was one thing Ernestine liked to do, it was play out all possibilities and have several options if things went bad. If she was one thing, she was a planner. And if things went 'to shit' as Robert was always saying, she wanted several options to be ready.

**

CHAPTER TEN

It's funny or maybe it's sad how true the old saying, "the more things change, the more they stay the same," was, Ernestine thought as she sat out in her backyard in cut-offs and an old flowered work shirt with the sleeves ripped off. Her thin black arms glistened with sweat in the sun.

The birds were whistling and singing all around her and it was the most normal sound she'd heard in a long while. She stretched back in her lawn chair with her combat boots propped up on another chair and sipped her Jack Daniels on ice with a splash of powdered lemonade. It didn't taste particularly good, but she didn't have many options these days. She was thankful she still had power. She was thankful she'd bought over thirty bottles of Jack before the world had all gone to heck. She was thankful the sirens had finally stopped and it was quiet and all she could hear were the birds and the occasional bee buzzing.

The past month had been one of sirens. Sirens in the morning and sirens in the night. As people burned and looted and crashed their cars and were chased by cops. As people tried to retain a grip on their city, on their neighborhoods or tried to leave the state. And through the whole civil battle, Ernestine sat it out, huddled in her basement, camped out on the fold-out couch where she had moved her tv and her computer and her landline which was actually on a long cord and was a heavy old phone from the 70's. She wanted a phone that would still work if the electricity was cut off and she wanted a corded landline because she felt it was more private to talk on than a cell just because no one used them anymore. Who would think to monitor it?

The power remained on and the phone remained on and the internet remained on if not a little slower. So the tv and the news remained on. Ernestine wasn't sure who the news thought it was broadcasting to but broadcast they did.

Thousands of townspeople voluntarily made their way to the university campus which was where the staging of the relocation took place the first week of August. That was when Ernestine moved her tv to the basement. Watching all the people voluntarily abandon their cars and walk to the university, carrying as many suitcases and belongings as they could, frightened Ernestine to death. What was even worse was when the news showed the searches of their suitcases. Watching the creation of a new authority right in front of her eyes on live tv scared Ernestine into a near mute state of panic. Relocation Services was their name and what their matching royal blue shirts all said. Were they from the water department? The police? The news reporters seemed as frightened of them as Ernestine as they tried to dig out the details without getting too close to the subject.

The news showed shots of the university quad set up in stations as people lined up for days to have their names checked off lists, to have their bags and boxes searched. All guns were taken immediately. Computers were examined and given back as were phones and other small gadgets. And then the people were all shuffled on.

Doctors examined them. Those with medical records and private insurance cards on hand moved on to a shorter line and those who didn't have them were moved to a much longer line and there the racial disparity was blinding. Short lines of white people with matching luggage and mass hordes of people of all colors carrying garbage bags of belongings lined up on opposite sides of the university quad. Some people were carrying gallons of water and drank from them in the heat but they had them taken away before being put on greyhound busses and taken away. The people without medical information waited and were slowly shuffled off to the big football stadium.

Ernestine watched this process for days and meanwhile she ignored everything around her during the day. She remained in her basement, paralyzed in front of the tv. But at night she took action.

She covered up her front windows with blankets. She stapled gunned them right into the woodwork around the windows. She had no need to look out front anymore, of that she was certain. She would have a better vantage point from the upstairs bedroom anyway.

She covered up her dining room windows as well but only with beach towels that she hung over the curtain rods. She felt she would want to be able to look out there from these windows. The backyard felt more vulnerable to her for some reason. As did the windows to the basement.

She oiled and opened and closed a window in the back of her basement till she was sure that it opened easily and silently. She put a stepstool under it so she could exit the basement by it without going up the stairs. She tried climbing out the window several times in the pitch dark while strapped with her two pistols. She tried climbing out it with a loaded rucksack full of survival essentials.

Then she walked around her dark yard and peeked in her own windows and tried opening them and the doors from the outside to judge how hard it would be to break in. Her yard was extremely dark when there was no moon. She mapped out places to put trip wire and she tried to do this the next night but it was so dark she couldn't work the wire and couldn't set the screws. She poked holes in her thumbs and fingers five hundred times with the sharp wire ends and was spitting mad and finally gave up and knew she'd have to do it during the day. She resigned to going inside and bandaging her fingers and that was when she realized she had left all her first aid supplies upstairs and hadn't put any in her rucksack.

The next day she ventured out during the day in the searing heat and strung her copper wiring four feet in from the back gate. Then she came back in and strung a trip wire at the top of the basement stairs and one across the middle of the front room. She wanted to be alerted by a falling thump if someone got in somehow and crept through her house. She wanted to be ready. What she would do if someone did come in, she didn't know. She prepared a fast escape by hiding a car key under the left front bumper of the car and she even stashed four boxes of ammo, several gallons of water and days worth of food in the car and then, heart pounding, she backed her car out in the dead of night with the lights off and turned it around so it faced nose out in her drive. She stashed a back pack under the car with water, a knife, first aid supplies and a lighter and a flare gun. She crammed this small black backpack behind the rear wheel. She didn't know why she left it outside the car when she had all the essentials in the car, but she did.

Ready, she said to herself a thousand times a day. Must be ready.

The second week in August was when the sirens began. Police sirens. Fire trucks. Ambulance sirens. The urge to drive around and see what was happening was overwhelming as was the urge to leave the state. But the news squashed that urge. Apparently the Relocation Services with the help of the police were rounding up all the people who had signed up for relocation and hadn't relocated. Those who had changed their minds.

"They came to get Pete," she whispered into the black handset of the phone down in the basement.

"Did he go quietly?" her mom asked and Ernestine felt all the miles in between them.

"He didn't answer. He wasn't there."

"Where'd he go? Did he get out? Is he hiding in there?"

"I don't know. They knocked and knocked and then just left."

"Were you hiding in the basement?"

"I was upstairs on the toilet. I saw the whole thing while I was on the pot."

At this, Ernestine's mother exploded with laughter.

"Oh Ernestine, you haven't changed at all."

"I want to come down there."

"No one in no one out," her mother reminded her.

It's what they heard on the news daily and nightly and what they heard on the boards.

"Sit tight," her mother told her. "Sit tight and let them round everyone up and then you'll slip down here, get on the blacktop from the forest, avoid the highways, take the smaller roads," her mother had planned it out for her.

Ernestine read the names of the towns along the minor highways as if they were the positive talismans they sounded like; Puxico, Ellsinore, Mountain View, Peace Valley, plus all the state forests and national parks seemed like a safe spot to stop and rest and find water from the pumps at the picnic areas and camp grounds. She hoped they were unguarded and empty. She hoped the small roads were clear and open. The Prius could not go off road with its little tires and weak engine. It could go far on a drop of gas only so long as the road was clear. She was ready to go but her mom kept telling her to wait; Utah was a crossroads for the military it seemed and her mother counted hundreds of military trucks a day from where she sat on the porch of her mobile home and watched them go by.

"I'm safe here, Ernestine. Foxy's is still open and I got plenty to eat and all the water I want down at the KOA. No one is bothering me, they think I'm a harmless old black woman," she chuckled.

Which was true. She was a harmless old lady. And that was why Ernestine worried about her. She wished she was down there with her, but she stayed put. She had fortified her house and she never went upstairs during the day now at least not for long. She slept most of the day. She cooked and used the toilet at night. And still the sirens screamed from around the city. Till finally at the end of August, it was suddenly quiet. She wondered where Pete had gone. She wondered what Robert was up to. One night when she went upstairs she pulled back the blanket from her bedroom window and peeked down at Robert's window but his whole house was dark. She went to her upstairs bathroom and peeked from behind the towels she'd hung over the blinds in that window and looked down at Pete's house but it was so dark on that side of the yard she could barely see his house.

"Did you put your sticker in the window?" her mother asked her and brought her back to the present.

"Are they doing that down there too?"

"I don't know. Not many people live around here. But I saw it on CNN that they're doing it nationwide. All the people who voluntarily relocated were supposed to put their sticker in their front window before leaving and those who stayed were supposed to put their sticker up so the government will know they're still there. Relocation Services said it was because the government still has a moral obligation to care for those who use their God given freedom to remain behind."

"That's bullcrap," Ernestine muttered.

She still had her green "Remainder" sticker and she still had a stack of red "Relocated" stickers on her dining room table. She hadn't put either up yet and now she was worried because what if someone came by to check on her already and they wrote down that she hadn't put up any sticker? Would she just put one up now and hope that that hadn't happened? Maybe so. But if she did, she'd put up a Relocated one. She didn't want anyone driving past to know that she remained. And if looters thought she'd be easy pickings, she'd handle them when they came a knocking or more likely, when they came a tripping on her wires.

"Labor Day is coming up," Ernestine said to her mom from where she sat on her bed in the basement.

She had hung a dark blanket in front of the one window but had taken it down to let a breeze in and had the window all the way open. The rest of the house was about 85 due to the ongoing heatwave and drought but the basement was about 70 and a breeze was actually coming in the open window. Ernestine had a few candles lit on top of the Ben Franklin stove to provide light. She didn't think they could be seen from outside in her back yard.

"Ayyuh," her mom said.

"Could get crazy on Labor Day. That's when people will do something."

"What people?"

"Whatever rebels are out there. Americans aren't going to stand for this relocation baloney."

"Americans lined up for this relocation baloney, dear."

"Whoever is still out there, the crazy rebels in this country. The nuts. The Republicans. The Libertarians, whoever those people are who shoot guns off and scare everyone on Labor Day. They'll unbury their guns and their rockets and their AR15's and whatever they got and they'll stop this."

"That's you Ernestine. You're one of the crazies with guns now."

"That's not me. I'm a progressive liberal. I never wanted any of this. I voted for Bernie."

"Ha! Don't say that out loud! Hahaha!" her mom laughed and then started coughing. When she finally quit she said, "Ernestine the crazy rebels who are left, who stayed behind, that's you. So you got nothing to worry about because you're just gonna sit tight a little longer and then make your way down here. It's safe down here."

"But when will I be able to get out of here? How will I know?"

But that was a week ago when sirens had been screaming day and night and there had been big police trucks roaring up and down her street. Now, it was suddenly quiet. There had been no traffic up or down her street for days. She could almost pretend things were normal as she relaxed back in her lawn chair and looked up at the stars. She wondered where Robert was. She wondered where Pete was and why more effort wasn't put in to finding him. Maybe things weren't as scary as she thought they were.

She went inside and up to her dark bedroom with her binoculars and peeled back the heavy blanket covering the window and then peeled back the curtain and looked down at Robert's house but all was dark. She could detect no movement behind the curtains.

Then she used the binoculars to look around Robert's yard. From the bedroom window she could see one side of Robert's house, part of his front yard and most of his back yard. Everything was dark and shadowy and nothing moved. She watched the shadows to make sure they all timed up with the trees swaying in the hot night wind. She was nearly in a trance when the trucks rolled up. Several diesel trucks from the sound of it, right in front of her house.

She dropped the curtain and blanket back in place and ran down the hall on tiptoe in her boots to the front bedroom and peeked out of the curtains down at the street. There were three Humvees pulled up, blocking the entire street right in front of Pete's drive. A huge group of men, dressed in black uniforms got out, three with a battering ram, and they charged Pete's front door. Ernestine dropped the curtains and hid pressed against the wall as she listened to them pound his front door down.

She slowly peeked out of an opening in the curtain as one man began yelling.

"We know you're in there! Come out with your hands up! We know you've been at the university! We saw you on camera! Come out and no one needs to get hurt!"

The men formed up in a column of two by two and with huge spotlights in one hand and black batons in the other, they charged in through the busted open door of her neighbor.

Ernestine moved to the bedroom behind the front one and peered out its long window as the men with the spotlights ran through Pete's dark house. She could hear them calling through the house to each other, their muffled cries of "CLEAR" came out of Pete's open windows. But no sign of Pete himself.

Ernestine's heart hammered in her chest as the men came running out of the front door even faster than they had run in. She leaned up against the wall and sucked in her breath as if they could hear her from outside. She was thankful she hadn't turned on any lights upstairs. She was thankful she hadn't left on any lights in the basement. And she kicked herself for drinking so much Jack that her reflexes were slow but all the same she knew that's what it would take to get her to fall asleep later, if these men ever left her street. She hoped they didn't do a door to door search of some sort.

She watched them as much as she dared as they swarmed Pete's front yard, side yard, his garage; as they searched every inch of his property. Every time they got near her fence she almost passed out and had to shut her eyes to stay calm. She was covered in sweat and was too afraid to wipe it away from her eyes. She was so afraid they would peek over the fence and see her pool glinting in the night; hear its pump filtering water, and that they'd be intrigued and come over to investigate. After all, it was very hot and a good night for a swim, she thought to herself and had to cup her hand over her mouth to keep from losing herself to a growing hysteria and laughing out loud.

Before the police swarmed Pete's house, because that's what she thought of them as, police, before they had swarmed Pete's house, she had started to get her nerve up and was thinking about venturing out into the neighborhood and maybe skirting the edge of the city and see what was going on. But after the police, even though she was fairly certain they were not police, after they had busted in Pete's door looking for him, she grew afraid again and took shelter in her basement where she had her bed and her tv and her phone and computer. She also had a large laundry sink and a Ben Franklin stove. She didn't have much wood down in the basement but she did have a camp stove and as long as the window was popped open, she could cook down there without killing herself. She still had to come upstairs for the toilet. And luckily the water was still on for washing and flushing. She could have drank it after boiling it but she chose to use her own water. After the police incident at Pete's, she ventured out of her basement less and less, until the cabin fever threatened to make her lose her mind. She was restless. She was lonely. She was tired of hearing her own voice in her head. She decided after several weeks of quiet, to go out. But she didn't go far.

"Robert," she whispered at her neighbor's back door.

She had taken her time going through his back yard. She had gone right over the fence, scaling it easy enough from her side and jumping down as quiet as she could on his thick overgrown grass. She had walked slowly through his yard looking for trip wires and booby traps but encountered none. She felt oddly exposed standing on his back porch as she knocked quietly. She hoped she wasn't frightening him by showing up so randomly and at that thought she had to stifle her laughing fit. She wondered if she weren't losing her mind completely.

"Robert," she whispered again and knocked harder.

She placed her ear to the door and listened and only heard the normal tickings of a quiet and empty home. She was counting her breaths and listening and thinking she'd give him twenty-five more breaths when she heard the door click three times and then open up.

"Ernestine, are you alone?" she heard Robert whisper from the dark.

"Yes, it's just me."

"Come in. Quickly."

Ernestine slid sideways into Robert's kitchen and blinked four times waiting for her eyes to adjust to the dark interior. On the fourth blink she saw his wide back descend down into the basement.

"Follow me. No lights," was all he said.

The basement smelled of socks and woodsmoke and beer and possibly a stopped toilet. There was a small camp lantern on an old dresser next to a beat up old couch covered in quilts. There was a cot pushed up against the wall with a sleeping bag and two recliners in front of a big screen tv that looked oddly out of place in the basement. Sitting in one of the recliners was Pete.

"Pete! You're alive!" Ernestine whispered in astonishment.

Pete looked to Robert and back to Ernestine and he seemed afraid.

"It's ok, she's alone. Come in Ernestine. We don't have to whisper but we keep pretty quiet."

"I haven't seen you or heard anything from over here," she said and sat down on the edge of the couch. She put her backpack of essentials on the floor between her boots.

"Look at you," Robert said and grinned at her as he sat in one of the recliners. "Locked and loaded," he said and let out a quiet whistle. He had a thick beard to go with his big mustache and he looked happy to see her.

Ernestine patted the 9mm on her hip and then reached across her body and touched the .38 strapped under her arm. She smiled and blushed in the dark basement.

"It's scary out there," was all she said and smiled again and it felt good to smile. It felt good to talk to another human.

"It is," Robert answered her and couldn't help himself but smile back at her despite the serious situation of things. "Did you see what happened the other night?" he asked her.

"The police?"

"Not the police, the Relocators."

"Yes. I did. They were looking for you," she said and turned to Pete. His glasses glared flat in the lantern light. "They said you had been at the university. They said they had you on camera."

"They'll be back," Pete croaked to Robert.

"They searched your house and your yard and I thought they were coming over to get me."

"They'll be back to get us all," Robert growled and reached over to a small fridge and took out a beer. "Beer?"

"No," Ernestine waved it away. "Why did you go to the university?" she asked Pete but he didn't answer.

"Tell her," Robert finally said as he cracked open his beer and sat back in his huge chair and chugged it down.

"I got my microscopes."

"I helped him," Robert added.

"You helped him? They'll be after you next."

"That's what we thought but they didn't see me. I waited in the truck in the cemetery."

"What did you find with the microscopes?"

"Our water is still fine," Pete declared flatly.

"Well that's good, isn't it?"

"No. The news still has reports of people dying all over the nation. Amoeba, bacteria, water catching on fire. Water being infected with attacking lice. And absolutely no water in California, Utah, Nevada," Pete said. He had no spark left in his face, no life in his eyes.

"Utah has water. My mom lives in Moab. She has water."

Both Robert and Pete looked at her like she was crazy.

"Are you sure?" Robert asked her.

"Yes. She goes down the road to the campground and gets it from the pump there. She uses their showers. She said the road is choked with Army," and here Ernestine couldn't go on for she was imagining her little old mother biking down the brown dusty desert road with Army trucks in order to go take her shower or get her water. Her mother was too old to be doing this, wasn't she?

"When's the last time you talked to her?"

"I talk to her every night."

"Your cell still works?"

"I don't know. I use my landline."

"You have a landline?" Pete asked incredulously.

Ernestine sat back further on the couch and tried to fade into the shadows.

"Yes," she said.

"That's fantastic. Can I come over and use it? I'd like to call my mother."

"Sure, Pete."

They sat and caught up on things for over an hour. Robert had a stash of Pepsi and beer but no water which was why he helped Pete break in and steal his microscopes.

"We just boil the tap water just in case and we're good," Pete told her.

"We're doing ok on food but we're not going to last forever. You got plenty?" Robert asked her.

"I'm good," Ernestine told them as she took the Pepsi Robert offered her. It'd been a long time since she had something so sugary and it tasted great. "I got lots of Jack Daniels," she offered up and then felt embarrassed for saying it.

"She does," Pete laughed and sounded like his old self. "I helped her carry in like forty bottles."

"You want to stay over here?" Robert asked her, his voice now serious.

"Why?"

"Well aren't you scared over there?" Robert asked.

"Maybe we'd be safer if we all stayed together," Pete suggested.

"No I'm fine over there," Ernestine said and sipped her Pepsi.

"How long do you think we can hold out here?" Robert asked and cracked open another can of beer.

"Not long," came from Pete.

"I want to go out and see what's happening," Ernestine told them.

"Not safe," both men said at once.

"I can't just sit here."

"We should go then. Me and Pete. You should sit tight," Robert said.

"Why?"

"Well. You know," was all Robert said.

Ernestine knew what he was getting at but didn't say anything for a while and she just drank her Pepsi and was quiet. They all were. It was nice that there hadn't been any sirens in a long time.

"You should stay over, sleep here," it was Robert who said this to her again.

"Am I keeping you boys up?"

"No. But doesn't it feel safer over here?"

Ernestine looked around. It was a lot smaller than her basement. And there was no fireplace and the window was small.

"Can you fit out that window?" she asked.

"I doubt it," Robert laughed.

"I can fit out mine."

"That means someone can fit in."

"I can fit in it. But I don't think a man could. I like to have a way out. I like my space too. I'm fine at my place. But you guys can come over. Call me on my landline maybe first because I got trip wires."

"Trip wires?" Pete asked.

"Yes."

"You," was all Robert could say as he smiled at her and wiped his mouth and beard on the back of one of his giant fists.

"I better go," Ernestine said and got up, causing both men to get up too.

"I'll walk you back," Robert offered.

"No need, I'll be quieter on my own," she told him and went up the stairs on light feet.

**

The next night she was reading the news on the boards on her computer when she heard a heavy thump by the back gate followed by another heavy thump and a man's voice cursing.

"Get off me, hippie," she heard Robert growl at what must have been Pete.

She peered out her propped open window and tried to see them but couldn't. She could hear their heavy breathing as they got up.

"We're going into town," Robert told her once she had guided him and Pete over the trip wire at the top of the stairs and down into her basement.

"When?"

"Tonight right now. Want to go?" Pete asked.

He looked silly and happy and Ernestine didn't mimic his mood at all but she was for it all the same.

"Yes."

"We're running low on things and we're plain out stir crazy and want to go see what's happening."

"Count me in. I'll drive."

"Nice, so we're storming the city in the vegan wagon," Robert chuckled.

"Hey it's silent," Pete chimed in.

"That it is," Robert agreed.

"Let's hit it!" Ernestine felt if she were going to go, she'd better go soon without thinking about it too much or she'd lose her nerve.

She led them upstairs over all the trip wires and out to the car where she retrieved the key that was stuck under the front fender. She grabbed the black backpack and threw it in the back, shoved supplies off one of the rear seats and opened it from where it had been folded down.

"Climb in," she gestured toward the car.

Pete got in the back behind Ernestine's seat and Robert got in the front and racked the seat all the way back.

"Women drivers," mumbled Robert as she pushed the start button and the silent electric engine turned on. She shut off the head lights and the dash lights.

"Make sure the dome doesn't come on," she told Robert and held her lighter up to it so he could see which way to slide the button.

"Good thinking," he told her.

"I'm always thinking," she mumbled and let up off the brake and rolled them out nose first into the street without a sound.

"Let's head north. North side has been evacuated longest," Robert said and pointed right.

"Take the main road?" Pete asked, scooching closer to the front seats.

"Sure, why not?"

"It looks empty," Pete said from where he was poking his head in between them.

"What's that sound?" Robert asked suddenly.

"The engine. The gas engine comes on if I get above 20."

"Oh."

"Should I keep it slower? It'll turn off if I coast too."

"No, just go normal. Maybe a little slower."

"It's so dark," Ernestine said as she sat closer to the steering wheel and strained to see down the dark four lane street that led to all the shopping.

"Where first?" she asked.

"I'm kind of hungry," Pete said from the shadowy back seat as they drove past the dark Arby's.

"The grocery store is furthest away," Ernestine said and couldn't help but sound worried.

"There's Tractor Supply," Robert said and chuckled from where he took up his whole seat and spilled over to the middle console next to her.

"Look!" Ernestine cried as she made her way carefully around an abandoned five car pile-up and an empty fire truck that looked blackened and burnt.

"That's ironic," Robert laughed.

"No, not that. That!" Ernestine said and pointed.

"Tim's," Robert mused.

She pulled up to the gun shop whose windows were all smashed out.

"Why we stopping here?" Pete asked. "Don't you people have enough guns?"

Ernestine and Robert both felt the pistols on their hips instinctively. Ernestine also had her .38 under her t-shirt that had a big kitten wearing nerd glasses on it. It said, "Are you kitten me-ow?" across the chest.

"We can always use more guns," Robert said.

The Prius rolled silently up to the gun shop whose windows were all smashed out.

"But it's clearly been looted," Pete protested.

There was gang graffiti tagged across the concrete walls of the front of the store and broken brown bottles littered in the doorway.

"We'll check it out," Robert said and got out of the car.

Ernestine turned it off and pocketed the key and followed him.

"See?" Pete exclaimed to them as they crunched over the broken glass.

Cloth gun bags had been ripped off the walls and thrown everywhere along with sunglasses and hats and other items. The glass cases and counters were all smashed out. It looked and smelled like someone had tried to start a fire in one corner. Packages of pepper spray were thrown all over the floor along with a few packaged pocket knives. The kind that had all sorts of attachments and came with a leather pouch. The looters must have not been interested in them at all. Ernestine bent down and picked up a couple.

Surprisingly, there were still several boxes of ammo stacked up neatly behind the counter. There were only a few brass casings on the floor and Pete kicked one and the sound of it rolling across the room rang out in the deafening silence.

"Stupid idiots left all this ammo behind," Robert said as he went behind the counter.

"See? No guns," Pete said and smiled.

But Ernestine walked past him and as she went she unholstered her 9mm.

"Ernestine," Robert called after her and set down his boxes of ammo he had collected and he followed her to the back.

"Anybody back here?" Ernestine called out, her voice wavering.

"Tim's at his trailer in the woods, remember?"

"I don't mean him."

"Oh. Right," Robert said and Ernestine heard the snap of his holster and of him drawing his weapon.

"Let me go first," he told her and edged his big bulk in front of her.

Ernestine couldn't see anything around him and felt frustrated at being behind him.

"Office is completely trashed. Dude," Robert said and stood aside so Ernestine could see the office had been ransacked hard. There was gang graffiti all over the walls, none of it legible to Ernestine. The Confederate flag was balled up in one corner of the room.

"See? Nothing here," Pete said and sounded scared from where he came behind Ernestine.

"Pete?" Robert said in the dark hall.

"Yes?"

"Go stand watch in the front."

"Yeah, Pete."

"Why?" he whined.

"In case someone comes in," Robert told him.

"What do I do if they do?" Now he sounded very frightened.

"Yell at us way before they get to the door," Robert told him.

"What do you have in mind now?" Robert asked Ernestine once Pete had gone back to the front.

"The safe."

"You think we can get in?"

"Yes."

"No way can we get in there. There's no way he left the combo here laying around," Robert said and gestured to the mess in the office.

"He did."

"But in this? We'll never find it. Will we?" Robert asked. He sounded amused.

"Nope. We won't," Ernestine said and holstered her pistol and opened her purse.

She took out her wallet.

"Give me some light," she said to Robert as they walked down the hall to the safe door which was the size of a double door.

Robert pulled out his lighter and flicked it near the small scrap of paper she held in her hands.

"What's that?" he asked quietly.

"Combination," she said as she entered the numbers.

"Must be a battery back-up," she said as the little key pad beeped and the door unlocked in several places and puffed open.

"Backpacks," Ernestine breathed out. "We need backpacks."

"Hell with that, we need duffle bags," Robert said and took off running back into the store.

He came back with six large rifle bags and two rifle cases that would hold multiple guns.

"Shotguns, Ernestine, get those on that wall, just the pumps," he told her and pointed.

She grabbed as many as she could as fast as she could and slid the long cold barrels into the bags, two in each, one right on top of the other, slid them in not caring if they scratched their stocks. She slid in two more and then two more and then turned around to look and see what else was in there. The vault was basically a room and it was wall to wall guns in the dusky dark.

Robert was breathing hard behind her and he was stacking up several skeletal looking rifles that all had straps on them for slinging over your shoulder. He looked like he was stacking branches, he had so many in his arms.

She felt like time was running out. They hadn't heard a sound from Pete. She hoped that meant everything was ok. She zipped up her bags after realizing she couldn't fit anymore and she tested their weight to see how many she could carry. It'd be good to get Pete back here to help carry them to the car. And then of course they'd need ammo. Lots of ammo.

"You ok?" Robert asked her in the gloomy room. He sounded winded and she looked to see he was shoving pistols in his pants.

She did the same, shoving two in the front of her jeans, under her billowy pink shirt, and then shoved two more under her belt in the back of her pants. She didn't know how she was going to bend over to pick up all the bags of shotguns.

"We done?" Robert asked her.

"Yeah," she said and blew a puff of air out of her mouth as she hefted two bags of shotguns up. "Let's get Pete to help," she said to Robert as he hoisted up his pile of rifles.

"Pete," Ernestine called out to the hall.

No answer.

"Pete!" Robert called a little louder.

Still no answer.

"That asshole probably went out to the car and is probably sitting there listening to NPR or something," Robert growled and started out the safe only to run right into Pete, who now wasn't alone.

"The hell this is?" a dark, young teenager yelled at them and shoved a gun sideways into Robert's face.

"Whoa, whoa whoa!" Robert yelled and backed up, stepping on Ernestine's feet as he did.

"Yo, the hell this is? Who the hell in here? This my safe mo-fo!" the kid yelled up at Robert's face.

Ernestine hid behind him for as long as she could and began to slide her 9mm out of her holster.

"Yo bish! Who back there?" the kid yelled and tried to shove Robert away but Robert's bulk was too much for him. "Wutchee doin' back there bish?" the killed yelled around Robert at Ernestine.

Ernestine was pulling her pistol up towards him, her finger sweaty on the trigger, ready to shoot him, yet scared of shooting Robert or Pete who were all jammed in close near the door of the safe.

"Get your hands the eff up bish!" the kid yelled at Ernestine and shoved his gun in her face.

"Rrrrrrrrrrrrrr!" a teeth baring roar burst out of Robert and he grabbed the kid by his scrawny shoulders and slammed him into the metal walls of the inside of the safe.

"RUN ERNESTINE! RUN!" he bellowed at her and she made to run with all the heavy pistols shoved in her waistband and one heavy long bag of shotguns in one hand and her loaded Ruger in the other.

"Run!" Robert bellowed again and shoved her from behind so hard she crashed into Pete.

Pete. Pete who was being held by two tall teenagers who now grabbed him by the arms and held him in front of them like a shield.

"Get in the safe!" Ernestine shrieked at them.

"Eff you crazy bish!" They yelled at her from behind Pete.

"No no no no no!" Pete was yelling over and over as they pulled him this way and that.

"Move mo-fo!" it was Robert. He reached right over Pete's head and grabbed the two punks and yanked them and shoved them in the safe where their friend was now getting up.

Before Ernestine could shove the safe door shut, the kid raised his pistol in that crooked slanted way he had of holding it. Without thinking, Ernestine raised her own straight up, a much faster pull than turning it sideways, and squeezed the trigger and fired off a rapid blam blam blam! At the kid and only stopped when Robert slammed the safe door shut.

"Arrrrrgh!" Robert yelled and started to shoot the keypad.

"No!" Pete yelled and put his hands over it. "They'll die in there!" he yelled.

"We gotta get out of here. There could be more!" Ernestine cried out and crouch-walked back into the main part of the store.

"We can't leave them in there!" Pete protested.

"We can't let them out!" Robert yelled back at him from behind Ernestine.

The main part of the store was empty and all was quiet except now, for the first time in months, a cool breeze was blowing in through the smashed out windows.

"We gotta go," she told them. "Grab as many shotgun shells as you can, I got two shotguns," she told them as she peeked out the door of the store and went to the black Prius as it sat in the parking lot. She hoped they hadn't done anything to the tires, but even if they did, she'd drive it home on the rims.

"Let's get the hell out of here," Robert said and sat down hard in the front seat, causing the car to dip a little. "Let's go Pete!"

"What's he doing?" Ernestine asked and pounded the dash with her palm.

"Probably trying to get those thugs out of there."

"I think I shot one," Ernestine told Robert and felt ill.

"The other two can snack on him then while they wait to get rescued," Robert said and pulled a cigar out of his shirt pocket.

"If Pete isn't out here in four seconds, I'm leaving," Ernestine said as she punched the power button and slid the selector into reverse.

"I'm coming!"

It was Pete and he was carrying a big heavy bag.

"What'd you get?" Robert and Ernestine both asked.

"Shotgun shells, like you said," he answered and got in the car.

"We left all those Ars in the safe," Robert said, and blew cigar smoke out the window.

"We left three kids in a safe," Ernestine reminded him.

**

CHAPTER ELEVEN

The house felt too small to Ernestine after they got home, especially with Pete who kept saying, "You shot that kid," over and over along with, "We have to go back."

It was because of this claustrophobic feeling that Ernestine suggested they sit out back. She couched it in that there was a strong cool breeze blowing for the first time in months and that she wasn't ready to be cooped back up in the basement.

"Speaking of being cooped up," Pete said as Ernestine brought out three glasses and a bottle of Jack to the patio.

"Shut up Pete. We'll go back," Robert said and threw back his shot of whiskey and then continued smoking his cigar.

The lawn chair he was in creaked under his weight.

"Good," Pete said and clasped his hands together. "Let's go!"

Ernestine gaped at him with a frightened look on her face. She felt frantic already and she needed it to end so she could process what happened and so she could just breathe normal for a bit.

"Sit down," Robert told him. "No one's going anywhere." Robert kicked an aluminum lawn chair at Pete with his big desert boot.

"But the kid is shot. He could be going into shock! Ernestine shot him several times even maybe," Pete cried, his eyes huge and his hands held out pleading.

"Stop. Please. I only wish she'd shot all three of them," Robert said with a curl of disdain on his lips.

Ernestine looked from Robert to Pete and then downed her whiskey.

"I'm going back," Pete said and the lenses of his glasses winked at them in the moonlight.

"So go," Robert told him and held out his glass for a refill from Ernestine.

"Ernestine," Pete said to her.

"What? I'm not going back," she said and shuddered.

"You'd let them die?" Pete asked, and puffed up full of indignation.

"No," she said slowly. "But I wouldn't go back tonight. I'd go in a couple of days."

Robert raised his glass to her and said, "Exactly," and smacked his lips.

"They could be dead in two days!"

"Just the one. The other two will be ok," Robert said and stuck his cigar in his mouth.

"That is not acceptable!" Now Pete sounded completely outraged and yet the more worked up he got, the more relaxed Robert seemed.

"That is not acceptable! It's Ernestine's problem!" Pete whisper shouted and emphasized her name.

Now Robert took his feet off the other lawn chair where he had propped them up.

"Stop making her feel worse than she already does. That kid had a piece pointed at all of us. She saved your life! And you were supposed to be the look out! Where was your warning?"

"I thought they were just kids!"

"Kids with a Glock!"

Ernestine felt sick. She wished they would stop talking about it and go home. In her mind, that kid was alive and ok. In her mind she had just made the choice between her life and his, and she chose her own.

"Ernestine," Pete now turned to her. "We have to go back tonight."

"I don't think that's a good idea," was all she said.

"Exactly," Robert agreed.

"Why not?"

"We can wait. And then we'll go back," Robert told him.

"I'm going now."

"You don't have the combo. Ernestine does."

"I don't. I don't have it anymore. I must have dropped it."

"Why did you do that?" Pete nagged.

"Because were in a fight for our lives!"

"We have to go back!" Pete cried, taking up his refrain again.

"We will. We need those guns," Robert said and then he looked at Ernestine. "Hopefully you dropped it out of the safe. But if you dropped it in the safe, we're all screwed."

"We should go back now," Pete said again.

"For the last time," Robert growled and gave Pete a menacing look.

"We should wait. We go back now, their friends could be there, looking for them. Looking for us. We could run into a lot of trouble,"

Ernestine's words raced to keep up with her mind.

"If their friends show up, maybe they'll find the combo and let them out," Pete smirked and crossed his arms over his chest.

"Better not. I want those rifles."

"We have enough guns, but all the same we go back tomorrow, because what none of us really want to do is have a few deaths on our hands," Pete started to sound preachy.

Ernestine was sick of his voice and she glared at him.

"Well we better get in the house," Pete said more quietly and stood up and handed back his un-drunk glass of Jack. "Looks like it's going to finally rain."

At that they all looked up and were amazed to see thunderheads gliding across the moon in the dark night.

Ernestine climbed into bed after Pete and Robert went home. She lay down with the window propped open and listened to the rain plunking on it hard and felt thankful to be safe at home. But she was still awake an hour later.

"It's still in the 90's here but that's better than it was," her mother had told her on the phone before she got into bed.

"It's dropped down to the 70's here," she had responded without emotion. Then she had told her she thought she'd be able to leave soon and get down there to her. She thought to herself now while she was in bed that she wouldn't tell Robert or Pete she was leaving. When the time came she would just go in the middle of the night.

She nestled down in the squeaky fold-out bed and breathed in the smell of mud and rain and envisioned the good sleep that would come with the cooler temperatures but yet she still couldn't relax enough to drift off.

She wasn't the only one who couldn't sleep. Robert was at her window after several minutes of tossing and turning himself. He whispered her name in through the open window just once and she jerked up on high alert.

"Psst, get up here. We're going to explore the neighborhood," he said in the dark over the plinking of fat steady rain on the downspouts.

She wondered how much rain was collecting in her barrels and remembered back to the day Pete told her they were illegal. She was so much more anxious then. Now that the world had actually gone to shit, as Robert was always saying, she was much calmer.

"Why do you want me to go?" she asked once she had gotten dressed. She had on her camo pants, black t-shirt, oiled monkey boots, and a camo rain hat with a wide brim. She also had her 9mm and .38 on, along with the survival knife she'd found on the floor of the gun shop and a can of pepper spray; all strapped to her belt.

"The more the merrier," Robert said and smiled.

Pete looked nervous and like he'd rather be inside and dry. The rain made loud splats on his black gortex jacket.

They headed out on foot, watching out for the trip wire on their way out of the gate to the front of Ernestine's house. It'd been forever since she'd been in the front yard. She paused as she stood in it and the three of them looked right and left before heading left. She glanced back at her dark house as they walked away; it was tall and dark and a part of her wished she was back inside it.

They walked on in silence. The street was empty. The houses were all deserted. They couldn't see much life at all in the dark rainy night.

"Jeez, I can't see anything," Pete complained and wiped at the lenses of his glasses with his thumbs as they set off walking past his house with the busted open door and across his front yard and on down the block. They stayed off the street, and they stayed off the sidewalks.

"Well? What do we do?" Pete asked as they stopped in the front yard of the first house they came to; a long, white brick home.

"We knock like good neighbors. But keep your voice down," Robert said.

The three of them stepped up on the low cement porch and Robert reached out and pressed the small glowing doorbell.

"It's weird that the power is still on, isn't it?" Pete asked. He sounded smiley and Ernestine had an urge to kick him, but reigned it in.

Her and Robert didn't answer him. Instead Robert pressed the doorbell again and Ernestine took a step back off the porch and rested her hand on her 9. She had a brief memory of trick or treating and it seemed like it was something she had seen on tv; her idyllic childhood was that far away from where she was now. She almost laughed in the dark but quelled it when Robert looked over his shoulder and asked, "What now?"

"Where's his relocator sticker?" Pete asked.

"Did anyone bring a light?" Robert asked and was answered by Pete pulling a short fat LED out and popping it on.

"Relocated," the three of them said in unison.

"Who lives here?" Robert asked.

"The man with the rubber arm," Ernestine answered without thinking and covered her mouth as if she'd said a profanity.

"What did you say?" Pete asked, outraged as Robert laughed.

"The man with the rubber arm?" Robert asked. "Jesus. Nice," he said and laughed again.

"Why did you call him that?" Pete demanded and Ernestine just shrugged.

"He was in an accident at the plant and got his arm mangled. He has a prosthetic arm, a cosmetic arm because he didn't have enough nerves left to use a robotic one," Pete said with a tight mouth.

"Who cares? I don't care if he has a cosmetic dick. Let's find a way in," Robert growled and tried the door.

It was locked but it was an old door whose hinges were sagging and only the door knob lock was locked. The door sagged so much, the deadbolt probably no longer lined up, and no longer would slide home in the jam.

"Stand back!" Robert ordered them and they did.

He heaved one thick leg up and kicked the heel of his right foot even with the doorknob and the great old doorjam splintered and burst open.

"Voila!" Robert grunted and they stepped inside and breathed in the scent of someone else's house.

"Jeez, I can't believe we're doing this," Pete complained as they looked around in the dark.

"Let's keep the lights off," Robert said as he led them forward to a kitchen.

It was small and orderly with white cabinets and a blue granite counter.

"Nice," Pete nodded his head in approval as if they were shopping for a home.

"All right ladies, let's see what we got," Robert said as they began to open cabinets.

"What are we gonna carry it in?" Pete asked.

Ernestine was silent and just went to the cabinet below the sink and opened it to find grocery bags stuffed inside grocery bags.

"Ahh," Robert smiled and began filling an IGA bag with can goods.

"Oh cling peaches in heavy syrup," Pete declared, "yum, I haven't had sugar in ages. And look, the good kind of peas, the French ones, and low sodium beans, these are good for you."

"Pete?"

"Yes?"

"Shut it."

"Thank God the power is still on," Ernestine stated, trying to alleviate some of the tension as she opened the freezer.

"We said that already," Pete told her as he peeked around Robert to see in the freezer.

"Frozen dinners, ugh," Robert sighed and moved on to the sink to bag the dish soap and matches and the dish cloths.

Ernestine shrugged and bagged the frozen dinners anyway then tied the bag in a knot and placed it on the oak dining room table.

"What do we have to eat at your place, Ernestine?" Pete asked as he sniffed a container of chocolate pudding from the fridge and began to eat it with his finger.

"We?" Robert asked.

"Yes, 'we'. We're in this together aren't we?" came from Pete.

"I don't know. Canned chilli?" Ernestine replied, as she dug through a junk drawer and pocketed some sugar packets.

"Rays?" Robert inquired.

"Yes."

"That's good shit," Robert said approvingly as he tied two heavy bags closed and put them next to Ernestine's.

"Let's look around," she suggested and set off going through drawers in a tall cabinet in the dining room. She bagged batteries and a couple of flashlights and two more books of matches that said, "I'd rather be in the Poconos."

"Where the hell are the Poconos?" Ernestine asked herself and tried to imagine the man with the rubber arm going to a beach and felt morbid and ashamed for thinking that.

Robert and Pete had moved on to the big family room that faced the backyard with large sliding glass doors. Ernestine took one look at these doors that faced the black backyard and felt exposed and wouldn't go in the room.

"We ought to come back with a wheel barrow or two and collect firewood from everyone. They're gonna shut the power off eventually and we could use it," Robert said as he came back into the dining room empty handed. "This guy has a huge fire place and a nice stack of wood in here. I bet he has a cord of wood out back," he pointed back over his shoulder. "You find anything?" he asked Ernestine.

Ernestine burned with embarrassment as she pocketed an ipod and headphones.

"An mp3 player," she mumbled.

"Cool."

"Let's check out his bedroom and bathroom and go," Robert said and then to Pete, "Hurry up!"

Pete came out of the family room carrying a big fleece blanket in his arms.

"What?" he asked.

Robert frowned at him and didn't say anything.

"You said it's gonna get cold, so I'm taking this blanket. I don't think Mitch would mind."

"Who's Mitch?" Robert asked and only got a petulant stare from Pete in response.

They bagged aspirin and Neosporin and hand sanitizer from the bathroom. They didn't find anything of use in the bedroom but a flashlight and a military novel that Robert pocketed.

"This guy is pretty bland, if I do say so myself," Robert intoned to Ernestine as they left his bedroom. "No booze, no guns, no girlie magazines, nothing."

Ernestine opened a closet in the hall and found several rubbery looking arms on a shelf above a shelf of towels and sheets.

"I take that back," Robert mused as he peeked over her shoulder.

"He was disabled!" Pete muttered as he came out of a second bedroom and saw what they were staring at.

"I have to hand it to him, he kept a neat house," Robert laughed and led the way back to the dining room table where they picked up all their grocery sacks and then stepped out the front door.

It was raining even harder now and Pete wanted to go home. They decided they'd take all the groceries back to Ernestine's and store them on her back porch for now. They cut through Pete's backyard and stopped at the fence between Ernestine's backyard. It was Ernestine's idea that they take some planks out of their fences so they could get to each other's houses easier and without going out front.

"Also, I'd like to take part of the fence down behind my house and keep my car parked over there in their drive. If they're gone, that is."

Everyone looked at the small yellow house behind Ernestine's yard. It was dark and quiet and you couldn't see much over the fence in the pouring rain. But someone could be there. Just like their houses were all dark and quiet but yet here they were. She looked at Pete and Robert and their pants and jackets were shiny and black with rain. She wondered what they thought of her idea.

"You're always thinking," Robert said and set his grocery bags down.

Pete did too. He looked tired and frightened in the pouring rain.

"I don't like ruining my fence like this," he told them as he stood there with his hands on his hips.

Robert ignored him and helped Ernestine take three planks down from her fence on Pete's side of the yard.

"We'll string a trip wire here, you'll need to remember it, but it'll trip up anyone else we don't want going through our yards this way," Ernestine had to almost shout to be heard in the rain.

Pete didn't like watching them take apart his fence and so he told them he was going to go load a wheelbarrow of his firewood up for them to store. He trudged off in the pouring rain to the very back of his own property to where he had a full cord of seasoned wood stacked. Robert and Ernestine had moved on to the back of her yard and were prying the boards off the fence. They were working together silently when they heard it. The unmistakable sound of helicopter blades chopping in the sky.

"Oh shit! Spotlight!" Robert uttered and shoved Ernestine through the opening of the fence in the back of her yard and on through to her neighbor's behind her. They ran through the yard to the back of the house where Robert slid like a runner into home plate and kicked in the basement window with both of his big boots.

"In you go!" he said and grabbed her shoulders and pulled her down on the muddy ground and slid her feet first into the basement.

She came out on top of a washer, right on her butt and slid off to the floor. Robert didn't come in as smoothly. He was a little larger. But he got in, and as he did he kicked the top of the washer and made a loud whomp as the metal of the machine bent in and then popped back out and echoed in the dark basement. He slid to the floor next to her, his big boots hitting the concrete next to her own feet. Then he grabbed her shoulder and pulled her into a squat as spotlights danced around on the muddy grass outside the window.

"Do you think they saw us?" she asked.

"No, it's too dark out there, too rainy and too much tree cover."

They waited on the basement floor, squatting, their muscles tense and ready to spring. They kept one eye on the open window and one eye in the direction of the basement stairs in case someone came down them. Ernestine pulled her 9. Robert did too.

The helicopter hovered above their yards; its spotlight played over their homes and their yards, cutting through the slick night. Finally it began to make bigger and bigger circles until they could hear it no more.

"I hope they didn't see Pete," Robert said in the dark and then he climbed up on the washer and crawled up through the window.

**

CHAPTER TWELVE

"I'm not just making trip wires," she told Robert the next day. He'd come out to see what she was doing.

It had stopped raining that morning and the sun had come out just as hot as before except now it was also very humid. Bugs screamed from all around. It was as if the world had been taken over by insects. The mosquitos were out even in the day.

"Car battery?" Robert asked.

"Yes, I'm attaching this car battery to this trip wire, so if you touch it, you're gonna get a good steady shock until you break contact. So pay attention when you come through here."

"Are you hooking batteries up to all of them?"

"This one," she said and pointed to the opening in the fence next to Pete's yard, "and maybe I'll do the one in the back. I only have one more battery."

"Where'd you get them?"

"I had them," she said and looked away from him, not wanting to make eye contact.

"Always thinking," Robert said and sounded impressed.

"Always thinking," she agreed.

"Anything I can do?" he asked.

"Nope," she said and clamped the battery to the wire and then stepped back. "Where's Pete?"

"He's in the basement; he won't come out because of the helicopter."

"Did he say anything about going back to the safe and getting the kids out?"

"Nope."

"Hmm."

"Exactly."

"We need to have a plan for getting them out."

"You want to go tonight?" Robert asked her.

"Well, how long can you go without water?"

"Three days. But we don't know when they last had water, do we?"

"So, tonight. We better go tonight."

"We need a plan first."

"I have one," she told him as she picked up another car battery off her patio and carried it back to where there was now an opening in the back fence going into the neighbor's behind her.

"Why did you want this opening? Remind me again."

"I'm going to park my car back here," she told him. "In their carport."

"Oh. Ok."

"Quit get away," she said to him as she went back to the patio and got the mallet and the tent pegs.

"Always thinking," he said to her again.

"Always."

"So what's this plan?" Robert asked as he took large strides to keep up with her.

"Help me string this tripwire and I'll fill you in."

Robert helped Ernestine do the labor of installing the tripwire and she filled him in on the details of her plan for getting the kids out of the safe without anyone getting hurt. Robert listened attentively as he drove the pegs into the ground on either side of the hole in the fence and then wrapped the wire around each end. He stood back when he was done and watched her clamp her battery to it.

"How do we test it?" he asked and smiled down at her.

"Touch it," she goaded him from where she squatted next to the battery and smiled up at him.

"Hell no, let's get Pete to touch it!" Robert said and laughed as they headed for the opening that led to his own backyard.

"That'll get him to come out more often," Ernestine answered and found herself laughing for the first time in a long while.

After it got dark they took a reluctant Pete with them to the north side of town back to Tim's Guns.

"I thought you wanted to get them out?"

Robert was craned around in his front seat and looking back at Pete who was sullen and quiet.

"Don't you care about them now?" Ernestine asked him and tried to look at him in the rearview mirror.

Pete was holding a plastic container with six fat homemade cheeseburgers inside.

"Oh my lord those smell good," Robert said as he sniffed the air.

"Thanks for lending me the ground beef," Ernestine nodded toward Robert as she drove down the empty dark road, past the five car pile-up that was still there and the burnt out firetruck.

"As long as the power remains on, we'll have meat about a year. My freezer is your freezer, we're in this together."

No one spoke as they pulled into the parking lot of the gun shop with the lights off.

"Lock and load," Robert muttered as they got out.

Pete was the only one without a weapon. He refused to use one. Ernestine had her two pistols on; the .38 concealed and the 9mm out in the open. She also had a pump shotgun in her hands. Robert had two 9mms strapped on him along with a pump shotgun in his hands too.

"You know the plan," Robert whispered.

And they did. They had been over it again and again as Ernestine cooked the hamburgers and had had to restart walking them through the plan over and over because Pete kept interrupting.

"What if the helicopter comes back?" he kept asking.

Finally, Robert had said, "Well we won't be home; they'll have to come back another time."

"Not funny."

"They won't be back," Robert had shrugged it off.

Now here they were in the dark with flashlights duct taped to the bottom of the barrels of their shotguns.

"Don't ever put the flashlight past the tube or it'll get blown to smithereens," Robert had explained when he helped Ernestine duct tape the LED light to her shotgun.

And now here they were with their shotguns loaded and their LEDs clicked on, ready to face whatever was waiting for them in the gun shop.

"Find the combo, open it up, they'll smell the food, we'll offer them water too," Pete chanted in a litany as they made their way to the door.

"Pete shut it! We clear the shop first, THEN find the combo," Ernestine whispered to him, not believing he was messing up the plan already.

They needed to go in completely silent, clear the building, find the combo, tell them to freeze, cover them with the shotgun, and then from there? She didn't know for sure if it would go right. They wanted to get them out on their faces, zip tie them and then they could get the rifles out of the safe. THEN they would give them a knife, leave the food and water and leave them.

Go in silent. Clear the building. Find the combo. Tell them to freeze. Cover them with the shotgun. Zip ties. Get the guns. Leave them the supplies and knife.

This is what she chanted as she watched Robert shoulder open the door into the dark gun shop. Now that it was raining out and there was little to no moon, the store was nearly completely dark with their LEDs lighting up parts of it in glaring, ghostly white.

Robert stepped in and slid with his back to the wall to the left, Ernestine came in next and slid with her back against the wall to the right. They hit the corners and the center and all the walls with their lights. Pete came in the middle, carrying the hamburgers and the zip ties, albeit he carried these reluctantly. Ernestine and Robert both had some themselves in case Pete completely lost it and was not there when they needed him.

Robert and Ernestine walked on silent feet through the store right down the middle of the floor and Ernestine watched as Robert sat on the wood counter and slid right over it on his butt and came down on the other side.

"Clear," he whispered to her and she went around the long way.

"Clear," she said as she checked all areas behind the three sided counter.

Next was the tight hall. There was no other way to do it but fast. Robert ran down it first and Ernestine followed right behind him, careful to not point her shotgun at his back. They passed the door to the safe, which was still shut, and they were glad to see that all was quiet as they went by. They continued down the hall and they stopped with one of them on either side of the door to the office. The door was closed halfway.

"Did we leave the light on?" Ernestine mouthed to Robert who just shrugged.

Ernestine listened hard. Her heart began pounding hard when she remembered there was no power on the last time they were there. She looked behind her back down the hall to see where Pete had got to. She was just waiting for him to make a loud sound. They should have told him to wait at the front door as the look-out but since he had flubbed that up so badly last time, and nearly got them killed, neither her nor Robert wanted to do that again. So they had just told him to follow them in. But he wasn't there.

Robert edged his big desert boot into the office and kneed the door open slowly. Desk, corner shelf, filing cabinet, floor; Ernestine and Robert's flashlights hit them all and all was empty. Except it wasn't. The mess that had been there the night before was somewhat organized, cleaned up. The Confederate flag was draped over the back of a chair. Drawers that had been ripped out of the desk were back in place. Papers were stacked. There was a camp lantern on the desk; its flame bright and steady and all was so quiet they could hear it burning.

Robert looked at Ernestine and flared his nostrils as if he could smell who was there, and who knows? Maybe he could. His eyes looked dark and fierce and the tendons stuck out in the side of his neck.

Ernestine felt a shudder go all through her, she was that scared and she backed up slowly back out into the hall one step. But as she stepped down there came a sound from the back of the building. It was the unmistakable sound of someone flushing the toilet and then the completely normal sound of water in the sink running. It was such a normal sound that it made it entirely that much more frightening.

Robert spun out of the office in a pivoting move that left Ernestine feeling clumsy as she followed him down the hall; their backs pressed to the wall as they went and their shotguns ready. They each got to one side of a closed wooden door just as the doorknob clicked and turned and opened slow.

"Freeze!" Robert barked and shoved his shotgun in the chest of the man as he stepped out.

"What's going on back there?"

Pete, who was still in the front of the store peeked his pale face into the entrance of the hall.

"It's Tim!" Robert yelled to the front of the store and his voice sounded too big for the tight area of the hall.

Ernestine wondered if the boys in the safe heard him. There went their element of surprise. She hoped there were no bullets in the safe to load up those rifles with. If there were, they'd be in trouble.

"What the hell are you guys doing here?" Tim asked after Robert put down his shotgun.

Tim was clearly shaken and his hand trembled as he put on his glasses and took a cigarette out of his pocket. Ernestine and Robert shared a look but neither one of them offered any explanation.

"Jesus, you scared me to death," he said and trailed smoke back down the hall where he went back into his office. "Look at this mess," Tim waved his cigarette around the office. "Frickin' criminals tore up my office. They'd have robbed me blind but the combo's not here."

"You leave the combo in your office, Tim?" Robert asked and smirked.

"I thought I had it with me when I went to the trailer. But when I got there, I didn't have it."

"I'm going to go check on Pete," Ernestine said to Robert and she gave him a hard look and then darted her eyes over at Tim who had collapsed in the office chair with a squeak of the springs behind his desk.

"Be right back," she said to Tim who just nodded at her and inhaled on his cigarette.

But Ernestine didn't go check on Pete. She went to the door of the safe. There were hundreds of receipts and old sandwich shop napkins and order forms and all sorts of papers of every size all over the floor. But she would know the piece of paper with the combo on it by touch because she had covered it with clear packing tape to protect it in her wallet. She ran her hands through the papers as fast as she could, feeling for it. She didn't want Pete to come see and she sure didn't want Tim to come see so she ran her fingers through them all as fast as she could while keeping an eye on the office door.

Nothing nothing nothing, she said as her fingers touched thin receipts and thin packing orders and thicker copy papers. Nothing nothing, napkins and more papers and not her taped up stiff little piece of notebook paper. Hers. Not hers. But she wasn't going to tell Tim she had taken it. And then her fingers rammed into the corner of it. Shoved it under her fingernail on her ring finger. The little taped up piece of notebook paper was shoved into a crack of the bottom seam of the safe wall. There it stuck curled up just a little. She pulled it out carefully and palmed and walked back to the office.

Tim was on a new cigarette which he held tight with his mouth. He had his glasses in one hand and his other was aimlessly rubbing his shaved blonde head. He stopped his rubbing and looked up at her when she stuck her head in.

"I'm going to use the bathroom, is that ok?" she asked him.

"Yeah, you don't look so good. You ok?" Tim asked her.

"I'm fine."

She spent about five minutes in the bathroom memorizing the combination. She had to. She thought about writing it on her hand but she didn't have a pen and couldn't risk Tim seeing it. So she said it over and over, staring at the numbers till finally it hit her.

She flushed the toilet and ran the water in the sink and went back to the office. Tim was telling Robert about the state of things in the state forest where his trailer was and now Pete was coming down the hall towards them with a look of confusion on his face. Ernestine shook her head no just slightly at him and prayed that he just kept quiet.

"Damn boy! You brought grub! Damn that smells good!" Tim interrupted his own long story on how things were nice and quiet out in the woods but how he was out of food and worried about all his guns. He stood up as soon as he smelled the hamburgers.

"Would you like one?" Ernestine asked him and picked one up gingerly out of the Tupperware. It was still hot and smelled garlicky and greasy and she handed it to him and tried to smile.

"So um Tim?" she asked tentatively as Robert shot her a look.

"Yeh?" he asked with a mouthful of burger and grease all over his chin.

"Did you have any luck finding your combination?"

"No, but I haven't looked through everything yet."

"Well," Ernestine swallowed. "Well. I think I remember it."

"What?" he asked and nearly choked on his food. He coughed several times and held his tattooed hand in front of his mouth as he choked.

"I might have seen it when you took us back there," and here she gestured at Robert, whose face was completely blank and Ernestine noticed that he would not look away from Tim. His eyes looked tense.

"What?" Tim asked again sounding even more outraged.

"I'm sorry. I tried to forget it," she lied and then was quiet as Tim tried to swallow a big bite of burger.

Ernestine didn't chance a look at Pete as he stood silent in the doorway holding the container of the rest of the hamburgers. She swallowed while she waited to see how Tim would react, to see how she should act.

"So what is it?" Tim asked.

"V-Day," Ernestine said. And then, "05081945."

"Argh!" Tim smacked his head. "I knew it was that but I put it in the British way," he said and smacked his head again. "I didn't want to get it wrong three times or it'd lock me out for 48 hours."

Ernestine didn't know what the British way was but she was glad to have solved this little prickly predicament.

"Were you coming back to get my guns?" Tim asked as he licked his fingers and stared hard at her and then at Robert. He had his glasses back on and they magnified his eyes.

Ernestine tried to smile again as she looked at him. She hoped she looked innocent.

"Maybe," she said. "But it was my idea because I knew the

combo."

"You gonna come into my house and take my guns?" he asked and his voice sounded silky and he made a show of flexing his arms and showing them his black zig zag tattoos that covered his pale skin as he pressed his palms to the desk.

"Dude. It's all gone to shit," Robert put in.

"We had a helicopter come at us."

It was Pete who said this from where he stood in the door. His eyes were huge behind his glasses and he tucked his grown out hair behind his ears several times but it wouldn't stay.

"Helicopter?" Tim asked and sat back down.

"We had a helicopter come in our yards. It was looking for me!" Pete said and sounded winded.

"He makin' this up?" Tim squinted his eyes and looked from Ernestine to Robert.

"No. He's not," Robert said and folded his arms across his thick chest.

"It was looking for you? How do you know that?"

"Because. I didn't relocate," Pete said and set the hamburgers down and looked dejected.

Tim squinted from Robert to Ernestine and he sat there and looked thoughtful for a minute before he said, "Did they shoot at you?"

"No," Robert said carefully, "but maybe that's because we all hid. But they were definitely looking."

"I thought they were going to shoot at me," came from Pete and it was so quiet everyone looked around for a minute as if to make sure it was Pete who spoke.

"The spotlights were intense, weren't they bro?" Robert spoke to Pete as if he were a scared kid.

Pete shifted uncomfortably from foot to foot and looked away.

"Well hell, let's get some guns!" Tim declared and kicked up out of his chair and strode off to the safe.

"There's one other thing we need to tell you," Ernestine reluctantly said to Tim as she touched his tattooed wrist before he could punch in the code to the combo.

"What?"

"There's three kids in there."

"There's what?"

"There's three punks in there," Robert stepped up level with Ernestine.

"What?" Tim couldn't believe what they were saying. He rubbed his palm over his head several times and then he pulled a gun from the back of his pants where it had been shoved under his belt.

"Ernestine shot one of them," Pete offered up and Ernestine glared at him.

"Good!" Tim huffed and began to breathe hard.

"We have a plan," she said and tried to calm him down.

"Frickin' hell, I have a plan!" Tim cried and tried to punch in the number to the safe but got it wrong and it beeped and flashed a red dot twice. "FRICK!"

"Let me do it," Ernestine said quietly and she stepped in front of Tim. "We ready?" she turned and asked Robert and when he nodded and raised his shotgun in the dark hallway, she punched in the combo slowly and stood back.

The little light turned green and beeped several times and when the door puffed open Tim grabbed it and slung it wide. Ernestine and Robert were side by side; one tall and wide and one short and slight, with their shotguns leveled at the occupants of the safe.

"FREEZE!" Robert yelled.

The three teens in the safe were lying down, curled up, and they moved slowly and covered their eyes to protect them from the bright flashlights. It must have been utterly dark in there. The fear they must have felt would have been nearly suffocating. Their eyes were crusty with tears.

They stayed on their sides and two of them covered their faces and grimaced; their teeth blindingly white in the glare of the LEDs.

"Nobody move!" Robert ordered them and then to Tim he said, "Drag them out, one at a time while I cover you, and you zip tie 'em."

Tim nodded agreement to this and shoved his pistol in the back of his pants and went into his safe which was a mess of rifles piled up all over the floor. He stepped over all the AR-15's and the shotguns and grabbed a kid by his elbow and drug him out of the safe on his side. The kid was all arms and legs and completely silent. If it weren't for his slow movements and his flexing fingers, Ernestine would have sworn he was dead.

Tim turned him on his stomach and Pete handed him zip ties and watched in horror as Tim bound the kid's wrists behind his back. Then he went back in the safe and grabbed another one.

"This one's cold."

Tim turned and looked at them, his face pale in the bright lights; and stated it matter-of-factly. "This one is dead."

He dropped the stiff arm and moved on to the other kid and hooked him by the crook of his elbow, untangled his legs from the body of the other kid, and then dragged him past all the rifles.

Once again Pete looked on in horror as Tim flipped the kid onto his stomach, pulled his arms behind his back and bound him. The kid groaned as his arms were pulled behind his back.

Robert was in the safe before Ernestine; feeling the kid's neck and rolling him partially over on his back. The poor kid was dead. Shot three times. Robert shook his head at Ernestine and motioned for her to stay out of the safe.

"You had to, Ernestine," he said to her as she drove them home later; the back of the Prius full of rifles and ammo and pocket knives and even cans of pepper spray.

Tim followed behind them in his truck which obviously had no muffler at all as it roared and blubbered and blatted all the way down through town.

"He's going to get us followed," Pete hissed from the back.

"He's going to help us stay alive," Robert corrected him.

They had left the two skinny kids bound with their hands behind their backs. But they hadn't left them empty handed. They gave one of them a survival knife. And they left them water and the hamburgers, now cold, and they also left them each a Glock and a box of ammo.

"We're all in this war together," Robert had knelt down by their heads and told them in a quiet voice.

"We're sorry for your friend," Pete had started to say and Robert knocked him away so hard he nearly crashed through a glass case in the store.

Ernestine said nothing. She waited in the car while the men loaded it up and then she drove them home. She parked in the carport of the house behind her and Tim parked his horrendously loud truck at the abandoned house next door to it.

"Watch the trip wire!" Robert reminded everyone as they headed across Ernestine's yard. Tim looked at the trip wire with the car battery rigged to it and smiled with admiration. They made their way silently around her pool and into her back door, each carrying an armload of rifles.

They made two more trips for the knives and the pepper spray and all the ammo. Just as they got in the house, it began to thunder. Ernestine went right to the basement and brought up a bottle of Jack and went right back outside to the covered porch and sat down to watch it rain.

"Now this is survivin'," Tim said as she passed him the bottle.

**

The question of the night, after they all got calmed down, was should they stay in town or relocate out to Tim's. Ernestine knew her answer.

"I'm not moving into a tiny trailer out in the forest," she told them but all the same she was thinking of her mom's tiny trailer in the desert.

"I think it's safer out there. It's hidden. It's dark," came from Tim.

Ernestine thought it was safer in town, nestled in between several empty homes, but she didn't say anything except that she was ready to go to bed and she wished them all a good night and then she went inside her back door and locked it and left the three men on her back porch.

Ernestine called her mom when she got inside.

"Have you seen the news?" her mom asked as soon as she picked up the phone.

"No? I haven't been watching tv."

"All state borders are closed, Ernestine. You'll never be able to get down here."

And it was true. On every news station she flicked to she could see how many of the states were trying to close their borders. No one in no one out. But not all of them. And not all parts of all of them. Northern Illinois was closed. Chicago looked like a zoo literally; they had erected tall fences around segments of the entire city with barbed wire on top and broken looking masses of people being herded and gathered by the military and by the cops as a handful of brave souls broke free from the group and tried to scale the fences. The border of Illinois was also closed all around St. Louis even though half the city seemed to be on fire.

But southern Illinois looked like nothing but trees and black top roads, open and unguarded. She saw a tiny glimpse of that part of the state when they flew in to show St. Louis. Otherwise they wouldn't have even shown it. The greenery of the National Forest made for a good contrast against the black and fiery footage of burning St. Louis. She could get out that way, she told herself. She could sneak out the bottom of the state through the forest roads. And that was the way she was planning on going anyway. She turned off her tv and fell asleep planning what she would pack in the car and when.

**

CHAPTER THIRTEEN

"Going on a run?" Tim asked her as she made her way quietly around her pool and back to the opening in the back fence.

It was still pitch black out at 4AM when she got up and snuck out of her own house to make a run to the overpass overlooking the highway that led into the National Park. She wanted to see if it was barricaded. She wanted to check it at different points from up high and see if there were roadblocks anywhere. She chose 4 AM because she had always heard that that was when people were their most deeply asleep.

She squinted in the dark to see him and saw a small green tent had been set up in the very back left corner of her yard, right near the electric trip wire she had set up.

"Yeah," she grunted and stepped over the wire and shifted her shotgun around in her hands and into the crook of her elbow.

"Want comp'ny?" he asked and stood up from the doorway from where he'd been sitting cross-legged in the door of his tent.

"Not really," she said and looked around to see if Robert or Pete was around, and she kept going through the fence into the neighbor's carport.

"I'm coming anyway," came from Tim as he fell in step behind her.

She heard the click and clunk of his weapons as he came quickly behind her and got in the front seat of the Prius next to her.

"This thing'll be good for runs cuz it's small and silent," he said and raised his eyebrows at her and she ignored him.

They drove through the silent, dark town, past the five car pile-up and the burnt firetruck and up onto the overpass.

She pulled up into the oncoming lane so she could get a good look over the railing and because there was absolutely no traffic it didn't matter what side of the road she drove on. The town was abandoned. Relocated. She stepped out of the car just a little and peered over the concrete wall of the overpass. She listened hard and heard nothing. No hiss of tires on the highway. No horns. No sirens. She heard the wind a little but only because they were up high. The frontage roads where all the Tire Barns, and Jiffy Lubes, the Lazy Boy store, the Dick Van Dyke Appliances, the Halloween Store, and the Bob Evans were all dark. For miles and miles she looked south and west and east and saw nothing but darkness and velvet black sky sprinkled with stars and she got back in the car and shut the door and drove away in silence.

Tim had stayed in the car and was leaned back far in the seat and smoking a cigarette.

"Nothin' huh?"

"Nothing at all," she said and her own voice sounded like a ghost to herself.

"It's that way for miles and miles. We could drive all the way down into Kentucky and there'd be nothing but black even though I bet those billys down there are still down there," he said and looked at her out of the corner of his eye.

She didn't say anything.

"We could go down there," he continued and took a drag on his cigarette and blew the smoke out her window into the rainy night, "and we could go to those caverns they got down there, and really hide. Hide really far away from everyone. One of them caves has a kitchen and even a toilet!"

"I wouldn't have taken you for the type of guy to hide."

"Hell."

He didn't say anything else but was quiet and thoughtful as she pulled a u-turn and headed south to the next overpass and pulled over again and looked out. Nothing for miles and miles.

"I'm not hiding," he finally said and flicked his cigarette out the window.

"You're not?" she asked him and caught herself turning on her turn signal out of habit and cussed under her breath and snapped it off.

"I'm survivin'."

"I don't need to hide in a cave. I have everything I need at my house."

"You do, but is it safe? Do they know you're there?"

Ernestine was quiet as she thought about that and as she took the back streets north through old neighborhoods of small houses some of which were boarded up and some that were burnt and charred. Wrecked cars threatened to block the road and she went around them carefully and cursed again that she had chosen this way to go.

"Watch out," Tim told her, "glass."

But it was too late as it crunched under her tires and she only hoped she didn't get a flat.

"Try not to brake," he told her as he stuck his head out the window and lit another cigarette.

"Why not?" she asked as she navigated around a compact car that had been turned on its side and smashed out of shape by what must have been a mob. She shuddered to think of what happened to the owner.

"Tail lights."

At that, Ernestine became very paranoid in the dark neighborhood that someone, maybe many someones were watching them coast by silently in the black little car. Maybe they weren't as stealthy as she thought they were.

"Just keep coasting. You're doing great, Ernestine," he told with the cigarette held between his teeth as he raised his AR-15 and pointed it out the window as they slid down to the end of the street.

Ernestine coasted up to the stop sign and did a quick look and rolled on through without looking.

"I felt like we were being followed," she said once they were a few blocks from the neighborhood.

"That's because we were," Tim told her and then climbed back into the back seat.

"What?" Ernestine asked and stared into the rearview mirror but couldn't see anything.

"Keep your eyes up front. I got the back."

She listened to him as he rolled down both windows in the back seat and she watched him as he kept his body turned to face the back of the car. All was dark in the street behind them.

"I'd really like to hit Tractor Supply, since we're close but I feel hincky about it with somebody following us," Tim said and climbed back in the front seat. He was of slight enough build to do that. Robert could have never fit back and forth like that, Ernestine thought as she took her eyes off the road to watch him get settled.

"You still see them?"

"No. They're gone."

"We could go by there. Case it out," Ernestine suggested.

"You trust leaving your car out front?" he asked and flicked his cigarette butt out the window.

"We could go in the store. With the car."

"What?" Tim asked and cracked a smile. "You got a plan?" he asked and couldn't help but laugh.

"Always."

Tim was silent as Ernestine cruised into the pitch black and nearly empty parking lot of the Tractor Supply store. She cruised the front of the store to double check that there were posts in front of the doors to keep cars from coming through; and there were. But that was ok. Ernestine had another idea.

She looped around the parking lot nice and quiet and slow one more time and then she parked far from the store, right next to the Wendy's, but kept the car running.

"You ordering?" Tim asked her and snickered.

"Nope. But let's sit tight a minute."

They sat shielded by the Wendy's on one side where Ernestine had pulled right up to the drive-thru window the wrong direction; in an even darker place than just the open lot in the moonless sky.

"No tail," Tim finally said. "No one moving anywhere."

"You sure?"

"Yep."

Ernestine pulled out of the Wendy's and headed back to Tractor Supply, across the lot where there were only a handful of empty cars parked here and there. She headed around the side of the store and to the back, to the auto bays of the oil change garage at the back of the store.

"We gonna get in there?" Tim asked.

"Yep. And then close 'em."

Three of the five doors were open. There was a pick-up truck up on the fork in one of the middle bays.

"Drive in, shut the doors, lock them if we can."

"Be better if you could back in," Tim said and squinted his eyes at her as if he were in deep thought. "Quicker get away."

"I don't think I can back in without putting her in the hole."

"Drop me off and loop around," he told her and he rolled out of the car silently before she was even at a complete stop.

She looped around the small lot of the automotive section with her lights off and kept her eye out for any movement around the garage doors. Tim ran in one and she watched as he stretched up and pulled it shut. He ran down to another one and shut it and then waved her to come in the last one that was still open.

She gave a furtive glance left and right before she eased the car in soundlessly. Tim had the door pulled down behind her before she got out of the car.

"I'm going to go out and try to open them from the outside," he called to her quietly and ran out a small door.

She heard him pushing on the door a few times and then he ran back in.

"This one has a bolt. And these garages must have a manual release in here somewhere."

Ernestine looked around the garage for movement. Then she handed

Tim two mags for his AR and she slung a pump shotgun over her shoulder.

"Let's keep the flashlights off," Tim said to her as they made their way to the garage lobby and through it to the door that led to the store. "I feel safer in the dark."

Ernestine followed Tim into the dark store. It was faintly lit by emergency lights flickering here and there at the ends of every fifth aisle or so. The store was hot and stuffy and smelled like tires and rubber and Ernestine's forehead was soon damp as she ran behind Tim across the store. She kept low in a crouch as they ran; weapons out.

"What a freakin' mess," Tim said when they got to the ammo aisle.

They picked through the boxes and bagged up all the shotgun shells they could find; loose and boxed. They also bagged other calibers they found such as hundreds of .22s and it reminded Ernestine of watching the news so long ago about the riots over .22s.

"Knives, we need knives?" Tim asked as he pulled one out of the package and ran the blade over his thumb.

Ernestine shrugged.

"We need food, and water," she told him.

"Meet you over there," he said as he began to open a package of camping matches.

"You think we should split up?" she asked and glanced around the dark store.

"Here, send up a flare should you get lost or get company," he said and sniggered and tossed her a flare gun.

She caught it on instinct and shoved it in the pocket of her hoodie and turned and left and went to find food. She grabbed a large duffle bag off the bottom of a shelf on the way and headed towards the registers where she knew the food was; where she and Robert had been when the power had gone out the last time they were here.

She had stuffed her bag with cans of soup and was moving down the aisle to the peanuts and salty mixes when she heard the smallest tiniest clink of a clip or a buckle of some sort hitting something metal. She froze with her head canted to the left, where she had been looking at the label of a salty peanut pretzel mix that was supposed to be spicy. She froze like that with her head to the side, listening to see if the metal tink would sound again. She was scared to blink. But then she did blink and it broke the spell and she pivoted on one foot and turned around to face the direction that she thought the tiny sound had come from.

She stood still and listened hard. She heard feet moving, almost shuffling, across the floor down one aisle and across from where she was. Someone was in the pop aisle. She heard cardboard ripping and then a crispy popping sound as a soda was opened.

Walk that way or walk away? Those were her choices. Walk towards it or away. Choose now. This is what she said to herself just before she walked toward the sounds. Shotgun up and pointed out, belly high to a man, flashlight off and duffle bag slung over her left shoulder. The shotgun wouldn't miss. Was she ready to shoot another person? Her finger rubbed the trigger and she knew the answer.

She heard feet shuffling and the soft wet sounds of someone drinking and then a belch; deep and long followed by a quiet laugh. That was when she peered down the aisle with her shotgun at the ready and saw him. He was almost half her age, barely old enough to drink beer, and he was about six feet tall and heavy, wearing baggy dirty jeans and a zipped up black hoodie with the hood on over his ballcap. He had a swollen black eye and several days of beard. He looked at her like he was too high to register that she was pointing a shotgun at him.

She started to speak. She started to say hands up. But just as she opened her mouth she heard a metallic click, a click she could have sworn she could taste, right behind her ear.

"Don't move," a silky voice said in her ear.

Ernestine froze with her finger still on the trigger of the shotgun. Shoot the pop drinker and spin? She asked herself but didn't have a chance to act because she was being told what to do.

"Lift the shot gun up, take it off and put it on the floor. Nice and slow," the man said with the pistol still pressed to the side of her head.

She glanced down the aisle at the pop drinker. He had stopped drinking pop and just stood there, staring at them. He looked fat and slow to her. He probably spent 23 hours a day sitting in front of a computer, moving his thumbs, drinking pop, eating junk. He probably had the reflexes of a dead man. She couldn't see the man next to her; she could see a vague dark shape, a wide shape, and figured he was just as fat and just as slow.

"Up, lady, get that shot gun up and over," the man said and poked her in the head twice with the pistol.

It was the second poke. It pissed her off and she thought, close enough to poke me, I'm close enough to poke you, buddy. It was then that she pulled the shotgun up as if to lift it over her head. The man seeing that she was complying took his pistol away from her head. She pulled the shotgun up as if to slip out from under the carrying strap but instead she yanked the stock of the shotgun backwards and up at the same time as she twisted hard to the right. She rammed the stock into the middle of the man's chest as hard as she could. She heard him cough and wretch and then she jammed him there again with the stock, just a short one. She felt the butt of the stock hit him in that hard plate of bone between his tits, and she felt satisfied at her own aim. And when he held his chest with his hand and worked his mouth in a silent "O" that was trying to get air in or air out and failing at it, that was when she rammed the stock of the heavy 870 shotgun in his bottom teeth, twice. Four short, powerful jabs; two to the solar plexus and two to the mouth was enough to get him to forget about shooting her in the head.

He held his mouth and then he cupped his chin as the blood began to pour out over his tongue and then he bent over and puked. She pried his gun out of his slick fat fingers and stuffed it in the back of her pants.

Now she turned to soda pop drinker. He was on the floor. She didn't remember shooting at him and her ears weren't registering any humming or whining so she didn't think she had fired the shotgun. Yet there he was on the floor; his feet were bicycling on the linoleum, trying to find traction. He looked like a fat cartoon and she fired above him into cases of soda and sent him scrabbling even faster. Now streams of rootbeer were fizzing up in the air and over him in hissing sprays. Finally he got his hands underneath him and got up and ran with his floppy old sneakers slipping on the tiles.

"Shoot, Ernestine, I told you to use the flare if you ran into trouble."

Tim came striding up laughing quietly, and when he got close to the guy who was still leaned over, puking up blood and spitting out his own teeth, he paused and looked at him.

"You know this guy?" Tim asked, rolling up the sleeves of his white oxford shirt he had on, revealing his black tattoos up and down his arms. He looked like a small, neat accountant who just happened to be covered in tats.

"Nah," Ernestine panted. "He put a gun to my head a minute ago." She shook and felt like she was going to puke herself. She had chills and sweats at the same time.

"Huh," Tim said and put his hands on his hips and twisted his lips as if he'd found a difficult problem to solve. "Well ok," he finally said and then he jumped backwards a bit and swung his leg in a perfect arc and kicked the man right in his bloody mouth and snapped his head back, before kicking him in the back, right above his kidney and collapsing him on the tile floor.

All was quiet after the man dropped to the floor. Ernestine listened hard to try and hear the fat guy who had run away. She strained her ears and listened for his shuffling clumsy feet but she couldn't hear any movement. She was mildly amused when she realized what she could hear was the store's speaker system, which must still have been running off the same generator that was running the emergency lights.

"Listen," she told Tim.

"To what?"

But Ernestine didn't answer, she just hummed to the speakers as they faintly played its canned music. She cocked her head; it sounded like George Michael's "Careless Whisper", the saxophone version.

**

"Always take Ernestine with you on a run," Tim said once they got back to the house.

"You didn't take me, I took you," she spoke up but was ignored by him.

Robert and Pete helped unload the back hatch of the Prius from where Ernestine had parked at the house behind hers. They had to tell Pete every single time to watch out for the tripwire. Even Tim, who had just started living in his tent in the yard, remembered the tripwires and where they all were. But Pete who had been there from the beginning had to be told every single time.

"Boy you get electrocuted, by God you'll remember to pick your damn feet up over that wire!" Tim goaded him.

They carried in all the ammo, snacks, soda, soup, water and more water, batteries, flashlights, lanterns, and a compound bow which Tim declared was a piece of shit and threw it aside as soon as he had time to sit down and examine it.

"Ernestine, she's always thinking," Tim said as he popped open a can of Orange Crush and sat down in a lawn chair.

And then he started telling them how she disarmed the man at the store and how she had lowered the truck on the fork in the garage at the store. How she had checked its oil and told Tim they should take it and load it up with as much as they could carry.

He was still going on ten minutes later but Ernestine didn't wait to hear what he said next because she felt embarrassed and she went into the house and down in the basement and called her mom. But there was no answer. She got on her computer, thankfully and miraculously there was still internet so she got on the Amazon boards to find her mom's posts. Her last post was from yesterday afternoon and it was for a Go-Pro camera though Ernestine doubted her mom actually filmed the little film with one. It looked like it was filmed with the cheap little phone Ernestine had bought her for Christmas two years ago; the one that had a keyboard that slid out the back for texting. It was about five years out of date but it was the one her mom wanted.

Ernestine clicked the white arrow to play the video and it showed the dusty brown road that went past her mom's trailer out in the desert. A light brown Humvee drove past and joined a line of several other dusty brown trucks raising up a dirt cloud as they went driving off into the desert.

"That's the last of them," Ernestine heard her mom say on the video. "They're all gone now," she said and Ernestine could hear the wind blowing into the little speaker. "It's just me now. I'm going to bike over to the camp tomorrow and see what they left behind. I'll post about it tomorrow."

And that was all she said.

Ernestine flicked through the boards some more, looking for sight of her mom but found nothing. She called her again on her landline. Then she called her cell. No answer. Nothing.

She sat with her head in her hands, sweat running down her face in a panic, trying to brainstorm what to do, trying to brainstorm where her mom could be. She was just about to sink into desperate thoughts and pure panic and scatterbrained plans of fleeing right now for Utah, when sounds of splashing and raucous laughter pulled her back to the present, to the basement where she sat. She pushed back from the desk and listened. Robert was yelling. Pete was laughing. And there was much splashing.

They were in her pool.

**

"Ernestine, try to calm down."

Ernestine was sitting in the dark on her back porch, stuffing her pipe, with her legs curled up under her in the lawn chair.

"Get away from me. Go back to your home!" she growled at Robert.

Pete had gone back to Robert's and Tim had retreated to his little tent in the corner of her yard after she had come upstairs from the basement and out onto the back patio and yelled at them to get out of her water supply.

"That's my water! We need that!" she had yelled at Pete and Robert as they stood there soaking wet in their street clothes in four feet of water which had always been smooth and only slightly rippling from the pump and was now tempestuous and slopping up over the sides, spilling onto the ground; the sides heaving in and out as if the whole thing were going to collapse.

"We've got water, Ernestine," Pete had said quietly and took off his wet glasses to wipe with his wet hands and Ernestine had just wanted to shoot him right then, she was that mad but he didn't even notice. "The water is fine, remember? We've been testing it."

"Get out."

And that was all she had said and she had gone back inside and locked up all the doors and gone down to the basement and sat in the furthest corner away from the stairs; back in the second room where all her water and food was stored.

When night had come she had ventured up and out. It was her house after all and she had to use the bathroom which was clear upstairs on the second floor. And then because the house was so hot and stuffy she had gone out back to smoke her pipe and unwind and get a little stoned before getting online and trying to find her mom again. But instead she had encountered Robert on her back porch. And he wouldn't leave.

"I'm going to leave soon," she finally said after they had sat there for a long time in silence; Ernestine finally went ahead and smoked and as she got more and more relaxed with every pull she took off her pipe, she stopped minding that Robert was there.

"You got a prescription for that?" Robert asked her.

"You gonna turn me in?" she asked and laughed out a long fluffy plume.

"No, just wondering."

"I grow my own," she told him and gestured to the back right corner of her yard with the pipe. "Back there," she said and waved her hand toward the sunflowers that were now bent over and dried out. "Back there," she said again and rested her head on the back of her lawn chair and shut her eyes.

"Good night for a swim," Robert said and caused her to open her eyes.

He was leaned back in his chair too and he had a cockeyed grin on his face. Ernestine watched a bead of sweat roll out of his short hair near his temple and glide down the side of his face.

"It's hot," he said to her.

"I'm thirsty," she said and started laughing uncontrollably despite her bad mood. Maybe she had smoked a lot more than she realized.

"No wonder," Robert chuckled and stood up.

He went inside her back door and came back out with a jug of water.

"Have a drink," he said and held out the jug to her but she was too stoned to hold on to it so Robert held it and helped her get a drink but she couldn't stop laughing.

"What's so funny?"

"My mom. My mom is not answering her phone. I have to go to Utah," Ernestine said and shook her head to get rid of the giggles.

"That doesn't sound funny."

"It's not. It's not."

"That's a long way to go, alone."

"I'll be ok."

"When are you going?"

"Soon."

"Go call her now."

"Now?" Ernestine asked and looked at him like he was crazy.

"Now, why not?" And he stood up again and now he was helping Ernestine get up.

"I don't think I can talk to her now."

"Too stoned?"

Ernestine didn't answer. She was ashamed.

"You sound fine. Just call her. I'll go with. You'll feel better afterwards. Then you can plan."

And Robert was right. She did feel better afterwards because her mom did pick up this time. And her mom did all the talking too, which allowed Ernestine to just sit and listen.

"What'd she say?" Robert asked after she hung up.

"She raided their camp after they left. She found mess kits and lots of water tanks and went back with her truck and took everything back to her trailer." Ernestine was in awe of her mom and couldn't get her mouth to close.

She had caught her mom on a return run from the Army camp and had listened in disbelief as her mom told her how she had scooped up all the leftovers from the camp. She had to go unload her truck and hide everything behind her trailer but she promised to call back the next day.

Ernestine just sat there on the edge of her fold out bed with her mouth hanging open.

"So, not going to Utah tonight?" Robert asked, smiling at her.

"I guess not yet."

"Good night for a swim. Might as well, Pete already had his hippy ass in it. You don't want to drink it now."

He was right. She did not want to think about drinking that water now. Her water. Her pool. She had stared at it out her dining room window all summer during the heatwave and now it was no longer pure. She looked out at it in the moonlight from where she stood in the dining room as she pulled at her braids and tightened them here and there and then dry washed her hands in disgust at her contaminated pool.

"All right," was all she said and she walked out back and climbed up the little ladder and got in her own pool, cargo shorts, boots and all. She collapsed backwards and sunk under the water and stared up through the bubbles at the black night.

"You finally got in," Robert said to her as she resurfaced.

It was like coming up out of a baptism when she stood up and looked at her backyard with new eyes. Or maybe she was just still a little too stoned, she thought to herself as she looked at the dining room windows from this perspective. They seemed to waver in the night. It must be the reflection of the water on them in the moonlight was the last thought she had as she was hit with a huge blast of air, noise, and glass and was knocked backwards into the water as the pool exploded all around her and she was swept backwards out of the collapsing, gushing pool and onto the cold muddy ground.

CHAPTER FOURTEEN

"STAY DOWN!" Tim yelled at Ernestine as she lay in the mud and completely voided her bladder as he fired his rifle from where he was crouched next to her.

She covered her head and tried to protect her ears from the deafening blasts from Tim's AR-15 on full auto. Her heart convulsed with every stream of shots and she was certain she was going to crap her pants next. She started to roll away from him a little, her arms still cradling her head, her hands covering her ears but recoiled and pressed her face into the mud because Robert was shooting now too and the blasts from his pump shotgun were even louder than the AR.

When there was a lull Ernestine crawled as fast as she could; keeping her ass down as much as possible. She wriggled her way back to the corner where all the sunflowers were bent over. Bullets were singing through the air and splintering holes in her fence; wood and hot casings were flying every which way above her head. And then it all stopped; there was no return fire and all was quiet.

She peeked out, saw Tim drop a fat magazine out of his rifle from where he squatted in front of his tent. She held her breath as he reached down in to a black duffel bag and felt around and finally grabbed another, shoved it home, pulled back the bolt and was up again. But now he was running toward the back of the house, crouching under the dining room window, which was all blasted out, on over to the patio and up on the porch and into the back door. He was so fast Ernestine had to do a double take to understand that he had just ran into her now bullet riddled house with an AR-15 hanging off his shoulder.

She sat up and listened from between the plants and flowers and heard nothing but a humming, whining, whistling in her ears. She watched as Robert, with his shotgun held waist high, walked slowly up onto the porch and he too disappeared into the back of the house.

She rammed her fingers in her ears and shook her head to try to get them to stop humming and then she got up, soaking wet from the pool, and now covered in mud as well, and walked to the back of her house.

"Um, Ernestine, you don't want to come in here," she heard Tim say from inside the house as she stepped up onto the back porch.

This warning just made her go in even faster. She only wished she had her guns on her as she stepped into the smoky house. There was glass all over the dining room table, floor, and it even reached the living room. There were huge bullet holes scattered up and down the walls behind the dining room table that she could fit her finger in, they were that big. She counted twenty-seven in one wall. Chunks of drywall lay gritty on the hardwood floor and crunched under her feet along with all the glass.

She peeked into the kitchen and saw that cups and plates had been hit and sharp white ceramic pieces dotted the floor. Part of the counter had been blasted away in small chunks. The front of the stove had several bullet holes in it. And there was a man sprawled out on the floor with a dark pool of blood growing from under him. She could smell it and she froze and stepped back into the dining room and called for Tim.

But Tim was no longer in the destroyed dining room, nor was he in the hall or the sunny living room. She heard the stairs creak and then she heard him running down the hallway above her and she saw Robert run up the stairs to follow him. She looked at the ceiling above her and followed their footsteps with her eyes as they ran from bedroom to bedroom, shouting 'clear' as they went.

"There has to be another one," Tim said as he led Robert down the stairs.

His eyes looked serious behind the lenses of his glasses and his jaw spasmed as it clenched as he looked around the front room. Dust motes swirled through the sunbeams.

"How'd they get in?" Robert asked.

Ernestine looked all around. The front door was locked. But something was wrong.

"The window," she gasped.

The blanket was gone from the windows in the front room. The glass was gone from one of the windows in the front room and it was sprinkled all over the blankets which were now on the floor.

"They just broke the window in broad daylight and came in?" Tim asked as he stuck his head out of the broken window; he poked his AR out the window as well, and looked all around on the ground below it.

Robert opened the front door and stepped out on the front porch and looked up and down the street for a vehicle but saw nothing.

"There has to be more than one," Robert said as he stepped back in the house.

"Ernestine, you recognize this guy?" Tim called from the kitchen.

When she got in there, he was nudging the man on the floor in the shoulder and rocking him back and forth. The dark pool below him was turning thick and sticky already.

"Is he the guy from the store?" she asked.

"That's what I'm asking you," Tim said to her as he stared down at the dead man.

"He's not the one that ran. Is he the one you took care of?" she asked.

"You mean the one I finished up after you took care of him?"

"Yes."

"I don't think so, do you?" Tim asked and looked closer at his face and then said, “He’s got all of his teeth, I don’t think we left the one at the store with all of his teeth.”

“It’s not him,” Ernestine said and shuddered and turned away and stepped over the trip wire at the top of the basement stairs and started down.

“Hold up,” Tim told her and got in front of her and went down first.

The fat guy from the store was at the bottom of the stairs. She knew it was him even as she saw him from the top of the stairs. He was dead apparently from tripping over the wire at the top and falling down the entire flight of stairs and breaking his neck. He still had his black and swollen eye that she had seen him with at the store and he still had on his hoodie over his ball cap too. She could see his one eye because his head was twisted strangely to one side, and his hat was tilted at an odd angle as well.

“This is the one who ran,” she said flatly and turned away from the dead guy.

“Yeh,” said Tim, “but who drove away?”

Ernestine grabbed her 9mm from where it was tucked under her mattress and ran to the back room of her basement with Tim right on her heels; where all her water and food were stored and where her water bottles were all now destroyed, shot up, and leaking all over the floor. Where a small basement window was busted out and where canned goods had been kicked down when the perpetrator had climbed up the shelving to get out.

“It’s not safe in town,” Tim said to her. “I should go home but I don’t like loose ends and I’m not leaving till we find this guy.”

Ernestine was silent as she stood in the puddles of water as she picked up a can of chili and found that it had several buckshot holes in it. She would have to go through all the cans and see which ones were shot up. And she would have to start hoarding water all over again because hardly any was left.

**

"Mom, I don't have enough water to even get me down to Missouri, much less all the way to Utah," she told her mom on the phone that night.

Her mom listened and Ernestine wondered how much to tell her without scaring her too badly.

"My pool is gone, my water supply is all gone. I should just head down there and figure it out on the way."

But Ernestine's mom was against that and she told her again and again to be patient; that she wasn't leaving Utah any time soon and that she was fine. She told her again and again to stock up her supplies and then get down there.

Her mom also told her that at least she wasn't stupid enough to try to find the guy who did this to her house, who shot at her. And Ernestine bit back the words she wanted to say to that.

Because they had gone out looking immediately. They had fanned through the neighborhood looking for signs of anyone who didn't belong there. Her and Tim went one way and Robert and Pete had gone the other; Pete only went because Tim goaded him.

Tim had gone on foot while Ernestine cruised the streets slowly and silently in her car.

"You'll be a sitting target in that car in the daylight," Tim had warned her but still she had gone in it.

"I'll loop around; I'll go ahead down the blocks and double back. But he's probably long gone," she had said to Tim as she buckled up.

She didn't think they'd actually find him and they didn't. She wouldn't have stuck around long if it had been her, that's for sure, she told herself as she pulled back into the carport of the house behind hers. There was barely any room in the drive what with the truck they had swiped from the Tractor Supply oil change garage.

"Give me the keys to that truck!" she told Tim when he'd finally caught up with her and come back to the house.

"What?" he asked. He had just lit a cigarette and was looking particularly angry at not finding the guy who had got away from shooting up Ernestine's house.

"They keys," she pointed to the little red and white pick-up.

Tim pulled the keys from his pants pockets and threw them to her.

"What are you lookin' for?" he asked as she dug through the glovebox.

"Registration."

She found a small plastic envelope and folded up in it were receipts for oil changes, a new muffler, car insurance ID and then folded up three times was a registration.

"Name and address right here. This is who did this," she gestured to her back yard which was now a muddy mess with the collapsed pool.

"You think?" he asked and took a long dry drag on his cigarette.

"I do."

"Let's get 'em," he said and ground his teeth.

"Let's at least visit," she muttered and scowled at her flattened pool.

"I like you Ernestine."

Tim was grinning at her as he cocked his head and looked at her.

"I don't like you, Tim," she said and walked away, making sure to step over her electric trip wire.

"How come?" he asked as he caught up with her.

"You're a racist."

"Have you heard me say something racist?"

"No. But look at you."

"We can't be friends because you think I'm racist."

"Look at me," she told him and stopped walking.

"What?" he asked belligerently.

"I'm black."

"I see that."

"And you're a Nazi."

"I'm not. I'm a skin but I'm not a supremacist."

"No difference."

"Big difference."

"Don't care," she said and started to walk into the back door.

"Will it make you feel better if I carry those bodies out for you?" he asked and grinned.

"Nope."

**

"If we're making a nighttime visit, we're all going," Robert said in the pitch black backyard.

Tim scratched a match on the brick patio and lit a cigarette and held out his mug for a refill on the coffee. It was 4 in the morning and Ernestine had woke up and brewed a pot of coffee to get ready to make her excursion as she called it.

"Excursion my butt. We're making a house call. We're goin' a visitin'," Tim nodded and said as he sipped his coffee.

"Drink up girls, we need to go while the goin' is good."

"Two cars, we need to take two cars," came from Ernestine. "In case they disable one of them," she added as she looked around into the faces of Robert and Tim.

Pete was still asleep in his sleeping bag in Robert's basement; unable to cope with anything and would not come out and talk with them.

Ernestine wanted to see who these people were, figure out if they were a threat to their future, and really just wanted to be back in her own bed, but glancing up at the now boarded up dining room window and knowing there was another one in the front of the house, she knew she had to act. She was almost killed in her own pool. Go figure, the first and only time she got in her pool, she gets shot at.

"We're just doing a cruise. We have to look and see what they're all about and then we come home and we make a plan."

"We gotta take care of them or we're gonna have to watch our back all the time," Robert said and cracked his knuckles.

"We know anyone on this block got a pool table?" Tim asked.

Robert and Ernestine stared at him like he had lost his mind.

"Why?" Ernestine finally asked.

"Want to make me a knock-out sock. Quieter than a gun."

"No, Tim, no."

"They come in handy," Tim said under his breath but no one paid him any attention.

"We'll take my car because it's quiet, and their truck, because it's theirs and it's a lot quieter than Tim's," Ernestine said to the men. "We can be ready to give it back to them for some sort of amnesty," she said tentatively as she looked at them to gauge their reaction, but they seemed more open to it than she predicted.

"What else?" Robert asked.

"I want to do two things on this run," Ernestine said to them in the quiet dark back yard, "I want to know who they are, get a feel for them, and we also need to do a water run."

Her heart had been hammering at a breakneck speed ever since seeing her water resources get completely obliterated in one fell swoop. She could not remember a time when she didn't have water. She still had some. There were older jugs of water in the back of her shelves that had not been hit. But nearly 50% of her water in the basement had been wasted. And all of her pool was gone. That pool was like a savings account. Like an IRA. A cushion to be used in hard times. And it was gone just that easily. She had never imagined someone coming to her house and shooting her pool like that. It made her wonder what else she hadn't ever imagined happening, that could happen. That could change her circumstances so quickly.

"So we're gonna do a recon?" Tim asked.

"Yes."

"We need to poke them to get them to come out so we can see them," Tim said, rubbing the top of his head as the thoughts formed in his brain. "We need to tickle the spider's web to get her to come out, you see?" he asked and took a slow drag and exhaled his smoke in the deep night.

"See," Ernestine said thoughtfully.

"She's always thinking," Tim grinned and nodded his head as if he could read her mind and agreed with her.

"Be right back," Ernestine told them and ran inside and down to her basement.

She came back up with a small duffel bag and handed it to Robert.

"This," she said shortly, "we use this; this is our element of surprise."

Robert looked into the bag and then looked back up at Ernestine, confused.

"Trust me, it's strong, point it at their door or their window."

"We need something before that, something to tickle their web as Tim said."

Ernestine looked around and then bent over and pried up a brick from her patio.

"Here, put that in the bag. That'll tickle their web."

"Always thinking," Tim chuckled.

"We need to be able to communicate." Ernestine sounded worried.

"I got walkies," Robert told them and placed two walkie-talkies on the patio table. "I'll go with Ernestine," he said and palmed one of the walkies and clipped it to his shirt pocket. "You go in the truck," he told Tim and tossed him the other.

"Channel two," Robert said.

"Let's go," Ernestine urged; suddenly anxious and ready, she stood up. She was pumped to get it done with.

**

"What are we looking for?" Robert asked her as they entered the neighborhood where the truck was registered to. "These houses all look the same."

And they did. They were all sprawling two story homes with three car garages. They were all half white brick on the first level with vinyl siding second floors and cedar shake shingle roofs. They all had huge paned windows with black shutters and yards that were still looked manicured even after being abandoned for a long time. Every single one had a steep driveway and a portable basketball hoop.

"Cherry Woods Vistas, what kind of douchebags live here?" Robert asked her as they slid silently down the curving road.

"Wealthy ones," Ernestine stated and strained her eyes to read the green street signs.

"This place is a nightmare."

"It could be a tactical nightmare to us," Ernestine told him.

"Why so?"

"We don't know the streets, they all look the same, at least to me, and there's dead ends everywhere."

"Cul de Sacs. The rich call them cul de sacs."

Ernestine just stared at him blankly for a second and went back to driving slow.

"Personally, I wouldn't live on any street called a 'sack'," Robert laughed quietly and rearranged his balls.

"Just tell me which way to go," she told him and pointed to the curvy map she had drawn on a piece of notebook paper.

Tim was way behind them sitting at the entrance of the neighborhood with his lights smashed out because they wouldn't turn off because of some automatic sensor or something, and he had the same hand drawn map so he could follow them shortly.

"Left up here on Orchard View," Robert said and pointed and Ernestine swung a soft left turn on the wide curving road. She heard Robert rip the top off the flare and throw it out the window. She watched it in her rearview mirror as it rolled to the curb.

"That was a good idea," Robert told her.

"I don't want to get lost in here is all."

They drove past the huge homes with the mailboxes out by the drives with the house numbers on them. Probably made it convenient for the mailman to just drive down the road depositing the mail. Some of the boxes were housed in their own little brick house and some were just plastic. None of them were bent or faded. It made Ernestine think of her mail slot and how long it'd been since she'd heard it flip flop open.

"Ok right here on Blossom Lane, and then a quick right again on Cherry Street, see right up there, right and right, God I'm getting car sick," he said and leaned out his window a little ways and chucked another flare.

"I'm coming in," they heard Tim say on the walkie.

"Roger that, look for the flares to help you see the turns."

"Roger."

"Ok Ernestine, Cherry Court coming up, it's a cul de sac on the left," Robert said and then got very tense and very still. "Drop me here," he said quietly and before she could roll to a complete stop, he was out of the car and she was still going on, past Cherry court as Robert ran in a crouch behind her car.

She went past the dead end, she refused to call it a cul de sac, and she did a u-turn in the dead-end a few houses down and circled back to where she had dropped Robert off. She couldn't see him. And she didn't have a walkie talkie and didn't have any idea of how he was doing. All she knew was he would open fire if there was trouble and she could decide if she wanted to come help or if she wanted to bail. That is what he had told her. She knew she would come help.

Robert was just a black shape moving up the steep front yard of the large two story home. He went halfway up the hill and she watched him reach down in the duffel bag at his feet and grab the brick. She counted her breaths from where she was parked nose out in the steep drive across the street as she waited for him to lob the brick. She wondered where Tim was.

The brick seemed to flow in slow motion across the yard and the crash was soft and watery sounding in the night. And here she counted her breaths again and waited for a response from those in the house.

One, two, three, four, five, six, and then the door whipped open and a man in long jean shorts and a Cardinals jersey and white slouchy socks came out on the porch holding a baseball bat.

Ernestine hurried and covered her mouth because she couldn't help but laugh a big loud spasm of a nervous cackle as she leaned on the steering wheel of the car.

And then Robert hit him with her ex-husband's old frog light. She could see Robert kneeling there in the dark with the huge spotlight held up high in one hand, blinding the man on the porch.

"Hands up now!" Robert ordered him and the man just stood there, shielding his eyes with one hand, the baseball bat still in the other.

"Drop the bat, bro!" Tim yelled from the dark as he came out from the bushes at the side of the house.

Before the man could drop the bat, Tim kicked him in the ass right off the front porch and into the bright light.

"Kill the light!" Tim yelled at Robert as he jumped with both knees on the back of the Cardinals jersey man and pinned him to the ground.

"What are you doing?" the guy yelled with his face now in the grass.

"We're taking a little walk and if you're good there'll be a consolation prize at the end of it."

"What are you talking about?" the man on the ground cried as Tim tried to bind his wrists behind his back but the man's arms were thick and he was squirming and fighting hard.

"We know it was you, asshole!" Tim yelled with his face down by the man's head as he tried to put all of his weight he could to hold the man down.

Ernestine strained to see what was happening from where she sat in the drive across the street but what she was seeing didn't make any sense.

The man on the ground whipped his head back in a brutal arc that caught Tim full on in the nose and eyes with the back of his skull. The blow was so destructive that Tim's head snapped back and he rolled off the man and rocked on his back on the ground, holding his face. Even in the dark, and even from that distance, Ernestine could see the dark blood oozing from between Tim's fingers.

"Robert, Robert," she whispered in the car to no one and banged on the steering wheel. "Do something, Robert," she pleaded.

But Robert was froze there in the grass on his knees as the Cardinal man crawled away a couple of feet and then picked up his baseball bat. He lunged to his socked feet and swung it, a big clumsy backhand at Robert and clipped him in the side of the head, spinning him around on his knees and dropping him there on the spot.

"NO!" she yelled in the car and slid the car into gear and rolled down the steep drive so fast she scraped the front bumper on the cement.

She rolled right up over the curb and turned parallel to the bottom of the steep grassy yard where Tim was now up on his feet, face covered in blood, black polo sport shirt tucked in neat and tidy and now shiny black in the dark night with his own blood as he reached one tattooed arm behind his back and pulled a pistol out of his waistband and in one fluid motion pointed it at the Cardinals man who had the bat coming back around to smack Robert again, as Robert struggled to come up on his knees.

Ernestine's mouth froze and her eyes stung from being held so wide open as she watched to see if Tim would stop the man before he hit Robert again.

"Mother!" Tim shouted and fired two rounds BLAM BLAM into the Cardinals jersey.

The man fell in a huge lump on his side with the dirty bottoms of his socks showing in the night.

"Get him down here!" Ernestine yelled out the window up at Tim. "Get him in the backseat!"

Robert was swaying on his feet and Tim grabbed the much bigger man by the crook of his elbow and yanked him down the steep yard and into the side of the little Prius, rocking it on its tires.

"Get in!" Tim huffed as he pulled open the back door and helped Robert crawl in onto the backseat. Then Tim looked up over the seat at Ernestine. "They're coming! There's more in the house! We gotta get out of here!" And then he slammed the door and Ernestine dropped it into drive and floored it and took off. She looked up at the rearview mirror and saw lights go on in the curtains of the house next door as they screeched away.

Their neighborhood, they know the way, look for the flares she repeated to herself like a prayer as she raced to the end of the street.

"Left off Cherry, left off Blossom, then take a right?" she said to herself as she navigated the wide curvy streets packed full of houses that all looked the same on streets that all sounded alike.

"Flare, there," she said, the tires of the Prius screaming around a corner and then, "flare there, now what? No flare. No Flare. Where is it?"

She looked in the rearview mirror and saw the moon glint off the black busted square headlights of the truck Tim was in was right behind her, right on her bumper. Keep going, she told herself, no time to turn around, there has to be another way out. Where is it? She let herself feel the neighborhood. The houses near the exit would have been the first ones built. Maybe had smaller front yards, maybe more bells and whistles on the houses to get people to come in and buy. Where were they? Shorter street coming up, named Cherry Vista, bingo, she thought to herself and whipped left. And there they were, three houses all on one side, all with blinged out front porches like no other in the neighborhood, and no houses across from them, just a small field across from them with the sign, getting closer now, Cherry Wood Vistas and the exit hidden by trees.

She gunned it out of the drive and took another left and got her bearings. This exit came out on the not so developed side of town. The side near the boy scout camp and the Construction Mining Truck Plant. CMTP. A huge complex, and then nothing but soybeans and corn for miles in all directions. Nowhere to hide. Son. Of. A. Bitch. Trapped, wrong way.

She gunned it down the black top and hooked a right into the factory parking lot, floor to the pedal and fifty miles per hour on a short stretch of black parking lot to the back of the plant, scanning now for a place to hide. The bald tires of the truck squealed and swerved behind her trying to keep up; Tim probably thought she was nuts.

"Hold on to something back there," she said to Robert and then, "Turn the walkie on for me!" and when she heard the click she yelled, "GO IN FRONT OF ME TIM! NOW!" and flashed her high beams on the gigantic garage ahead of her at the end of a row of closed huge garage doors, and prayed like hell that a 20 ton truck was not parked on the other side or they'd both be applesauce.

CHAPTER FIFTEEN

"Roger that," came from the walkie and Ernestine watched as Tim roared around her in the big truck, black smoke trailing out of it as he gave it all he had.

Tim looked like he was going to hit it so hard he wouldn't even be able to stop once he got in there. She squinched her eyes half shut as she followed him towards the door.

The white door exploded all around the truck and large pieces of aluminum flew ten feet up into the air as the truck disappeared into the dark factory.

Ernestine braced herself as a sharp piece of door came swinging down onto the hood of her car with a squealing shriek and flying of sparks and flew off like a metal wing as she gunned it into the dark opening of the factory. She flipped her lights on as soon as they got in because it was completely dark and she knew Tim didn't have lights on the truck anymore. Then she flicked on her highbeams and slowed down to get a better look all around because the place was cavernous and nearly empty.

Tim, however, wasn't slowing down, he drove on down past row after row of boxes stacked up clear to the forty foot ceiling. He kept going and now he was finally slowing down as they came up on a long line of twenty foot tall yellow dump trucks, parked end to end for as far as she could see. She flashed her brights twice and went around Tim and led the way down the trucks.

She parallel parked the Prius behind one of the trucks when she found two that were spaced out far enough, and she killed the lights.

"What now?" Tim asked when she got out of the car and walked up to his window.

"I think," she said and realized she was out of breath and could hardly talk. "I think we should leave like my dome light on in the Prius and then get Robert and me in your truck and go a ways away and stake it out. We won't be able to hide your truck in between 'em; it won't fit. But we can set a trap for them, if they follow us this far, then we can pick 'em off, I guess."

She leaned over with her hands on her knees and took a few deep breaths and looked left and right and listened hard for the high squealing of tires on the slick floor and heard nothing.

"Help me get Robert out," she said to Tim who was still sitting in the cab of the truck.

"I'll get Robert. You get your guns and any identification from the glove box," Tim told her.

She left the glove box open after taking out all the registration and insurance cards and stuffed them in her hoodie. The little light was like a beacon in the nearly pitch black factory. But yet it wasn't bright enough to show them anything, and they would have to get close to check it out.

"Park the truck nose out," she told Tim, "And we can just ram out another door and get out if they come after us."

"You stay in the truck with Robert," Tim said to her as he lifted him up into the crew cab.

"No, I'm coming with. I got your back," she said as she slung her shotguns and her black backpack with water and snacks in it onto the seat of the truck.

"Even if I am a Nazi?" he asked and grinned at her, his face coated with dried blood and his eyes already turning black and swelling up from the headbutt.

Ernestine didn't answer him, she just flipped the safety off her pistol.

"Just kidding, Ernestine. People joke, you know," he said and held his hands up.

"I know. That's what they tell me," she deadpanned, and then she smiled at him, a smile that didn't reach her eyes even as her teeth shone white against her dark skin.

Ernestine and Tim split up and each took a vantage point where they could keep an eye on the Prius. Ernestine's point was standing behind the front wheel of one of the twenty ton trucks. She topped out at five feet tall and the tire she stood behind was at least three feet taller than she was. She could stand under the wheel well easily without fear of bumping her head on anything. She picked a truck across and down from the Prius just a little bit. She wasn't sure where Tim went. She listened for him. She listened for the sounds of a vehicle entering the huge facility and heard nothing. She edged her nose just beyond the huge tire, keeping an eye on the dim light coming from the Prius in the dark, and she suddenly yawned and leaned on the big tire. She was exhausted and just wanted to be home in her own bed but she didn't know if she'd ever feel safe there again. She strained to see where Tim was, or at least to hear where he was but she heard nothing. She raised her 9mm all the same and braced it on top of her wrist and pointed it at the little black car.

They stayed there for an hour. It was so dark she felt like the outside darkness was seeping into her eyes, filling her up. She was dead on her feet tired and she was also worried about Robert who probably had a concussion from being hit with the bat.

She whistled long and low and was surprised when the whistle came back from about nine feet high and across from her. Tim was up on the staircase leading up the side of one of the huge trucks. She saw him when he stepped out a ways from the yellow truck.

"They're not coming," she said and gave up her position. "Let's check on Robert and head home."

"Your call," was all Tim said.

**

"We should go back to that place sometime," Tim told her once they got home and got Robert down his basement stairs and tucked into his bed.

She checked his pupils with a flashlight again and again to make sure they were dilating right. He kept telling her he was fine but she was very worried about him taking such a hit with the baseball bat. She found him some extra strength pain pills and got him a bag of ice for the lump on the side of his head.

"It looks worse than what it is," he told her again as he leaned down to the little fridge and pulled out a beer.

Ernestine watched in silence as he chugged the can of beer, belched a few times and then lay back with his eyes shut. He groaned each time she lifted his eyelids but he kept telling her he was going to be all right.

"I feel like crap, but just let me sleep, I'll be fine," he growled at her.

"What do you want to go back to the plant for?" she asked Tim as she finally left Robert to go get some rest. Pete had promised to keep an eye on him and she trusted him to make sure Robert didn't go into a coma.

"I don't know, might be safer than here," Tim shrugged and looked around.

"We need to make a water run," she said as they slogged past where her pool had been.

"That too."

"We need to sleep."

"That as well. I got a bitch of a headache," Tim said and rubbed his swollen nose tenderly.

He had two black eyes and his forehead was bruised and swollen and his nose was certainly broke but Tim had said it was no big deal; that it had been broke before.

"Shouldn't somebody keep watch while we sleep?" Ernestine asked as she looked back at Robert's house where they had left him snoring on his back, his thick chest rising and falling slowly and his mouth falling open just a little.

"I'll take first watch," Tim offered. "First let me make some coffee," he said and headed up the stairs of her porch to help himself to her coffee machine.

Ernestine went upstairs instead of heading down to her basement to the room where the man had fallen and broken his neck. She headed upstairs to her bedroom for the first time in months and crashed into her own bed into the deepest sleep she'd had in a long long time.

She woke up seven hours later with a wild rush of blood to her heart and a squeezing in her lower back which she was certain was her adrenal gland straining to shoot out a load of adrenaline to get her going because it must have heard what her unconscious brain didn't hear.

Flip-flop.

The mail slot.

HELLO REMAINDER! We see that there is a firearm registered to you. We will be in YOUR NEIGHBORHOOD SOON to collect all firearms.

Ernestine ran back upstairs and dug out her kitty cat jogging suit once again and then set off to the basement to get the ammonia.

CHAPTER SIXTEEN

By the time the Relocation Services as they were called, showed up to her door to collect her registered firearm, Ernestine had been wearing the jogging suit with the cats all over it for five days. She also hadn't showered in that time. She also had done her hair in five odd sized braids with kitty cat plastic barrettes. She also had had time to fill litter boxes with pure ammonia throughout the house, in case they also wanted to do a search. But most importantly she had also had time to get Tim and his tent out of her back yard along with all of his weapons, and her newly acquired shotguns and unregistered 9mm and all the boxes of ammo purchased and looted, all out of her house and off her property.

They ran it all down to the house that had once belonged to the man with the rubber arm, as Ernestine called him and Tim accepted it as such and Robert didn't comment as they made a 3AM dash down there to stow it all. They also stowed Pete down there because he was supposed to be relocated and not a remainder. Robert also disappeared, along with Tim for those five days, presumably out to Tim's trailer in the woods, but they didn't tell Ernestine. They just gave her a cell phone number and said to call when the coast was clear.

She was nervous as hell when the Relocation Services men showed up to her house and it lent itself to her act as she invited them into her house with an over the top trilling laugh.

"I'm actually glad you're here," she said and took them into the kitchen where the smell of ammonia was its strongest and the green flies buzzed around five day old bowls of crusty tuna remnants.

The men in the navy blue uniforms looked angry and nervous as they followed her into the house and they held their noses and coughed at the warm, still, stink that lingered heavily in the house.

"It's been so lonely since everyone left, you know?" she asked them as she removed a plate covered in foil from the counter. "I've made cookies, and I have rice milk for everyone," she smiled and blinked several times at the men as she offered them grainy, seedy, thin cookies she had made out of bird seed and wheat flour and cut with cookie cutters.

"Ma'am, we're just here to get your firearm," said the overweight one, the one with the flushed red cheeks and the sweaty hair. He looked to be in his twenties and his stomach overflowed his pants and strained the buttons of his blue shirt.

"Oh, oh, ok," she said and she had to fight hard to keep any anger or resentment out of her voice because not even deep down, but actually simmering right on top, she was very mad at giving up her firearm that she had purchased.

"Ok," she told them and led them back through the house to the stairs. "It's upstairs, can you come up and get it?" she asked them and wrung her hands together in front of her five day old jogging suit that was covered in playful kittens.

"No ma'am, we cannot come up and get it. You were supposed to have it ready for transport. You were supposed to have it unloaded and boxed up and ready to hand over."

"Oh my. Well. I don't like to touch it, you see?"

At that the two men frowned at her and didn't say anything.

"Ma'am. Get the gun," the skinny one with the curly hair and the Elvis sideburns told her.

He looked impatient and disgusted with her.

She ran up the stairs and back to her bedroom where she kept it in the box it came in. She opened the box and thought about loading it and shooting them. Robert knew she would have that thought and he had warned her to keep her cool and just hand it over, play the part of crazy cat-lady and get them out of there without further impression of her. And with his words echoing in her head, she shut the box and carried it back downstairs.

"Am I to get anything in return for turning this in? Do I get it back someday or a check for its value or at least something?" she asked and at the end of her question an edge crept into her voice and the skinny one shot her a look as he took the box from her.

"No."

That was all he said but he stared at her for an entire minute as he held her box in his hands like he was holding a small pizza.

"No," he said again and flared his nostrils at her and then glanced around her house and sniffed and sneered at her.

Ernestine's heart ratcheted up so fast and so hard she was worried she would start hyperventilating or even pass out. She felt very unsafe here in her home without any weapons with these two men. She wanted them to leave; now. But the skinny one just stood there, glaring at her, his nostrils flaring in and out as the fat one grew uncomfortable and shifted his heft from foot to foot in her front room.

Finally the skinny one cocked his head and took a deep breath and Ernestine took a half step towards the front door and gestured at it. But he didn't move. Instead he opened the box with her .38 in it and he took it out and popped open the cylinder and looked through the holes.

"Bullets?" he asked her.

She only shrugged and said, "He wouldn't sell me any because his shop was actually closed when I got there to pick up my gun."

"Michael?" the skinny man asked his friend.

"Yes?"

"Take her down."

The fat man looked at Ernestine and back at the skinny man and his face bloomed two red spots up high on his cheeks and he said, "Ok," in a high voice and stepped forward in his huge black shoes and swung his fat arm in a wide horizontal arch and swatted Ernestine in the side of her face with his thick, fat, enormous hand. Her teeth klocked together and her nose popped and she spun around and felt very dizzy and then she saw the hardwood floor rush up at her as she dropped like a limp sack of potatoes in a small heap in her kitty cat jogging suit on the floor.

Pete was crouched behind the bushes of the little house across the street, eating noodles out of a Styrofoam cup and waiting for the men to leave Ernestine's house so he could call Robert on his cell phone. He paused mid slurp of a curly noodle as finally the screen door opened and the skinny man came out followed by the bulky younger guy who was now carrying a limp and curled up Ernestine in his arms. One of her house slippers fell off as he carried her to their utility truck in the street. Her eyes were shut and her mouth gaped open and was bleeding as she lay small and limp in his arms. The big man held her out away from his body as the skinny man wound duct tape around her wrists before they placed her in the back of the big truck.

Pete realized he was dripping soup all over his leg as he sat there in the bush watching it all happen with his mouth hanging open. The two men got in the front of the truck and drove off, leaving Ernestine's white house slipper lying on its side in the dirty street.

"Jesus, Mary, God, Jesus, Mary, God," he said over and over as he dialed the little cell phone to call Robert. "Pick up, please," he said but the phone beeped after five rings and a detached voice said, "The number you have dialed is out of range of cellular service," and Pete hung up before letting it say more and he got up and ran to Ernestine's house where the door was still open.

Pete ran through her house in a blind panic and then he remembered her car parked at the house behind hers and ran back there; slipping through the muddy circle where the pool had been and back to the opening in the gate, and he actually remembered the trip wire and vaulted over it in his moccasins. He felt around under the rear bumper of the Prius and found her key and while bending over he found what she had called her 'jump bag' behind the back wheel. He grabbed it up and put it on the passenger seat next to him.

He stared at the dashboard and the square plastic key for a second trying to figure out how to start the strange little car and then finally saw the slot where the entire key was to go, shoved it home and pushed the start engine button and pulled out of the drive and went to find the Relocation Services truck.

Pete hung back from the truck because the roads were completely vacant of traffic and he didn't want to be noticed at all. Luckily they drove in a straight line and headed south down the four lane road. Pete pulled over and watched them go four stop lights ahead, way ahead past all the subdivisions with "Shire" in their names; Devonshire, Ayershire, Greenshire, Briarshire. And then they turned right and headed west on an industrial road that headed past strip malls and a winery and ended at the dog park and the water treatment plant.

Pete eased the little black car away from the curb and gunned it up to sixty down the road and swung a hard right and slammed on the brakes once the truck was in sight, three lights ahead on the empty road. He watched them go two more lights and when they crested the hill and then dropped out of sight, he punched it again to catch up.

The smell of waste floated on the hot breeze as he came down on the other side of the hill, as he left the strip malls behind, the semi-detached town homes and the Walgreens. The dog park was coming up next and after that would be the water treatment center which odd enough was just a half mile from huge new homes starting at the low $400,000s. Who would want to live way out here by the poop factory? Pete asked himself as he watched the truck turn in to the water treatment plant.

The dog park offered no cover, but there was a small trailer home park right before it and he slid the little black car in there and drove down the winding roads till he made his way to the very back of it, to be as close to the dog park as he could get, so he could see the water treatment plant. But all he could see was the big truck which was now parked near a square building, in between three huge round water treatment tanks.

The smell was oppressive as he rolled down his windows and dialed the little cell phone again.

"Yello?"

"Robert, it's me! They got Ernestine!"

And so Pete filled Robert in four times, explaining everything he saw. No, there were no gunshots. No, there was no fighting. No, he didn't think she was sick because they had taped her hands together. No, he didn't see them carrying anything else out but Ernestine.

"Robert, we're wasting time! What are we going to do?"

"Are they still there?"

"As far as I can tell. I mean, the truck's not left, no one has left. They could be killing her!"

"Get in there Pete and get her!"

"I can't, how? I don't have a gun? I don't," Pete stuttered into the phone.

"Tim and I will load up and be there in an hour, so keep your pants on. We'll get her back," he said at last before hanging up.

While Pete waited on the other two he went through the backpack he had grabbed. He dug through it and found water, a knife, first aid supplies, a lighter and a flare gun. He fiddled with the flare gun and pointed it out the windshield and pretended to fire it several times. Pete had never fired a real gun and he hoped he never had to. He stuffed the flare gun into his cargo pocket on the side of his leg and hoped it didn't go off accidentally and at this he had a moment of hysterical giggles. Finally he got himself under control and he started going through the medical supplies. He drank two bottles of water while he waited on Robert and Tim and by the time they arrived, he needed to take a leak.

"What's the plan?" Pete asked them as soon as they pulled up in two trucks; one quiet and the other, Tim's, very loud.

"Did you look in any of these trailers?" Tim asked as he looked around.

"No, why would I?"

"Could be people still in some of 'em. These are the types who would remain," Tim said as he looked around at the little metal homes.

"Why would you assume that?" Pete asked and took off his glasses and began wiping them on his shirt.

"These people been through some shit, obviously. Look at how they live. These little things are tornado and fire bait. But these folks live here. They're tough. They're not going to relocate when water gets a little short or nasty. Hell, they live next to this stench," Tim said and tilted his head towards the water treatment plant.

"Let's see if anyone's home," Robert said and grinned.

"Why? Why would we do that?" Pete asked, sounding panicked. "We're supposed to be rescuing Ernestine."

"We will. But it might be nice to have one of these as a hideout after we get her."

"Why wouldn't we just take her home?"

"Have you seen the roads around here?" Tim asked.

"Yes. I drove here," Pete said, looking at Tim out of the bottom of his glasses.

"Then you know that once you're on the road, it's all open. There's nowhere to hide. We have to be thinking ahead, like Ernestine would do if she were here. And this is where we hide. Right here."

"Let's try this one," Robert said after peeking in the windows of a trailer across the street from where they were parked. "I like this one," he said as he wiped the grime off one of the windows and peered in. "Two doors on this side and one on the other. And it looks empty. Let's go in."

They did a quick recon of the little trailer that had a small wooden porch built around one of the doors. There were pots of dead geraniums and other plants all over the deck. Inside the kitchen everything was decorated in black and white cows. There was a handmade quilt on a fairly new sofa and one of those Art Linklater chairs that would lift the sitter up into a standing position with the pull of a lever. There was also a pair of small light blue quilted house slippers next to the chair as if the owner had just stepped out of them.

The place was empty.

"This will be our hide-out," Robert said as he opened and closed kitchen cabinets and found a bottle of unopened prune juice and a large unopened jar of applesauce.

"Old people food," Tim said.

"Yep."

"Where's the vantage points? We might have to defend this

place."

Robert ran his tongue all around his teeth under his lips as he thought about it for a bit. Pete helped himself to the bathroom where he relieved himself for two whole minutes.

"The roof," Robert finally said. "One of us lays down on the roof with a rifle and keeps a lookout."

"Me. I'll do it and if they come I'll cover you while you get her in the truck and get out of here. Pete will have to drive while you keep your tail covered," Tim said and looked up at the roof of the little trailer home.

"It's a go; let's get Ernestine back, now."

"What's the plan?" Pete asked as he came out of the bathroom. He smelled like Dial soap.

"We go in the dog park, I think, and come in that way," Robert said and looked at Tim.

"It'll be dangerous going over the fence on the other side. I don't like it. We go behind the dog park, looks like just flat prairie out there but there's that hedgerow, see?" Tim asked as they walked back to where the trucks and the car were parked.

"Skirt along there?" Robert asked and pointed to the tall pussy willows and cattails that grew in a clumped line behind the dog park.

"I don't like snakes, and that looks like a place for snakes," came from Pete.

"Quit being a pussy, we're saving Ernestine from these jokers," Tim snarled at him and handed him a pistol.

"Oh no," Pete said and held up his hands. "I don't do firearms."

"Take it you dumbass," Tim snarled at him and shoved it into his side and let go of it, making Pete have to grab it.

"Where do I put it?" Pete asked quietly but no one answered.

"Here," Tim said as he opened a small round black can. "Rub this on your faces," he instructed them as he smeared a thick dab around his own face.

Robert smudged his face with the black shoe polish and handed the can off to Pete who smeared it on his forehead and cheeks and then just dropped it in the grass as he ran to catch up with the other two.

The hedgerow at night was an itchy, loud, cricket filled, scratchy mess to get through in the dark. The edges of it were damp with the rain from the past two nights and the men squelched through it slow and easy. Tim never took his eyes off the water treatment plant, which was getting louder and louder the closer they got. Robert kept looking back at Pete, whose moccasins were soaked and about to come off, and who kept swatting at mosquitoes and cussing under his breath.

They didn't make the quietest most organized or sneakiest arrival, but no one seemed to notice them just the same.

The stench was overwhelming in the humid air; you could almost taste it and feel the greasiness of it on your lips when you were right up close to it. And the noise was a nonstop ruckus of agitators and churners and water being forced here and there and sludge and human waste being filtered out and spun in centrifuges. There were warning signs and notices everywhere they looked when they got close to the huge square building. Tim went first up to the door. He had a high powered 30.06 slung over his shoulder and his 9mm pistol in his hand as he went up to peek in the square little window at the top of the door.

Robert and Pete hung back behind the big utility truck in the parking lot and waited to see if it was clear to enter. Robert pulled a large knife out of his waistband and rammed it in the front tire of the truck and then sheathed it and ran to Tim at the door. Pete slopped behind him in his wet cowhide shoes; he turned back to see the truck listing low to its front corner where the huge tire had quickly deflated.

They opened the heavy red door to a long metal staircase that went immediately up. It would be noisy but again there was so much noise coming from all around them that they doubted anyone could hear them if they took care to go slow and not bounce the metal stairs. But Tim pointed up to a corner by the door where there was a small black camera. If they'd been seen, they'd been seen already. Robert walked over to it and looked in it with a fierce scowl on his face and then reached up and ripped it off its mount. Tim looked at him and away and then back at him; he didn't think it was the smartest thing to do but now it was too late. Now, if whoever took Ernestine looked at their screen, they'd see nothing but black screen or static instead of an empty hall.

Tim held up one finger and told them to wait and then he tiptoed up the stairs on light feet without a sound and when he got to the top he waved them to come on up.

When they got up the stairs they saw tall white tubes around three feet in diameter that reached all the way to the twenty five foot high ceiling. They were making loud humming noises and they had ice formed at the bottoms of them that dribbled down the sides and pooled onto the floor all around them.

"The heck is that?" Tim asked.

"Liquid oxygen," Pete said and went on to explain, "They pump that through the water during the last process of putting ozone in the water, you know bubbles, to give it a final,"

"I don't care!" Tim cut him off and hushed him. "Shut it and fan out."

They split up three ways and made their way through the long hall of tubes of liquid oxygen. The deeper they went, the stronger the foul smell of human waste filled their noses.

"Jesus, I didn't think it could get worse," Robert waved the air and squinted his eyes against the stink.

Now they were passing long rectangular metal containers and could hear water rushing through them, up and down and they could hear trickling sounds multiplied by the millions. But no one was in the room.

Onward they went to the next room of large containers with a thousand pumps running and the sounds of thick sludge being pumped into Olympic pool sized vats that stretched out in front of them.

"Oh shit," Tim grimaced and held his nose. He leaned over and glanced down into one and gagged and wretched. "Look at that, shit, it's actually shit and, and, hair, euugh," he said and he spit a huge glob into one of the vats.

"I don't think she's this way," came from Pete. "Why would they have her this way? We should turn around." His voice sounded watery.

"We've gone this far, we're going all the way to the end before we turn around," came from Tim as he pressed on and ran on the narrow bridge that went over one of the pools of human waste.

Their feet tinged on the metal bridge as they went across it and their eyes bugged out as they looked left and right and forward for anyone coming out after hearing their approach but no one did. After they crossed the pool and were heading for a dirty yellow door in the brick wall opposite they heard a dull tinking sound coming from behind them.

"What is that?" Robert asked.

The three men looked from side to side at the five huge pools of brown greasy waste and listened for the sound. And then they heard it. It was a weak almost metallic sound; it was the sound of something soft and small striking a hollow railing.

"Over there, on that bridge!" Tim said and took off running to the pool furthest from them.

When they got to the end of it they looked down it and in the middle there was Ernestine laying down on the bridge on her side, bound to the railing by her hands. She had duct tape wound around her head and across her mouth. Her eyes looked wild and panicked and her hair was coming out of its braids and flying all around. She was struggling against the tape on her wrists but was only making it pull harder.

Tim was by her side immediately and with a glint of a blade he had her released from the railing with a quick slice and then he had the tape off her wrists. She immediately pulled at the tape around her head.

"Wait, let me," Tim told her and he sliced through it at the back of her head as she held very still and as soon as she heard the slice, she tore at it and ripped it off her face herself.

"Huuuuuuh," she panted and took a huge gulp of air and wiped at her runny nose with the back of her hand.

"Ernestine, what happened?" Pete leaned down and asked.

"Those bastards," Ernestine gasped.

"You can tell us later, let's get you out of here," Robert said and leaned down and grabbed her hands and pulled her up and helped her steady herself on her socked feet.

"Where are they? Do you know?" Tim asked her.

"No, I don't. They just brought me to this shit pool and taped me up and left me a few hours ago. They said they had to call someone and ask them what to do with me." Ernestine looked around and seemed frightened and small in her kitty cat jogging suit. She didn't seem like the Ernestine they had come to know in the past few weeks.

"Here," Tim said and handed her her own 9mm and then pulled his rifle up to his shoulder, ready to fire.

"Let's bug out," Robert said and led the way back over the bridge, back the way they had come.

"How many of them were there?" Tim asked as they ducked back through the door that led to the rectangle containers of rushing water.

"Two. There were two."

"A big one and a skinny one," Pete added.

"Any more since you got here?"

"No. I've only seen the two. No one else," she said as she ran next to Tim with her pistol firm in her hand and raised up and ready to go. She wanted to shoot these guys. Both of them; even though she suspected the fat one was actually ignorant and innocent, he had backhanded and for that he was going to get shot, she decided.

They ran past the rectangular filters and on into the room with the huge frozen tubes of liquid oxygen where there were warnings of no flames and warnings that the tubes could explode because they were under pressure and highly flammable.

"I want to find them," Ernestine said in a raspy voice as she pulled on Tim's wrist. She nodded at him with a vengeful look on her face and he looked down at her small black hand on his pale white tattooed arm and he nodded back.

"Let's look for them then," Tim said and tilted his head towards the heavy door in the brick wall across from them.

"In there or up to the next level?" Robert asked.

"Might as well look in here while we're here," Tim said and walked toward the door.

"Why are we even looking for them?" Pete asked. "Why aren't we just getting out of here?"

"Shut it Pete," came from Robert and Tim together and Tim opened the door.

But it was an empty office with two metal desks facing each other and nothing else in the office but a printer and a bookshelf built into the wall. Empty. All three men stepped in to look when it was not necessary. Ernestine lingered behind them with her back to the stairs leading up to the third level. She was tired, she was in shock, she was aching all through her body, she was mentally done as well.

"Hey! Who the hell?" they heard someone shout from behind them. The skinny man who had kidnapped Ernestine had just come down the stairs from the third level. "How did you get in here?" he demanded as he came down the stairs with Ernestine's .38 special in his hands.

"Weapons down, all of you!" the skinny man demanded as he grabbed a dazed and tired Ernestine around the neck and put her own .38 up to her head.

The three men rounded on him with guns raised except for Pete who seemed to not have his pistol anymore. He groped in the back waistband of his pants but came up empty and when he realized that he took a step back behind the other three as he ran his hand down his leg to his cargo pocket.

"You'll be putting the gun down, bro," Tim said and took a step towards the guy with his rifle raised.

"Oh jeez, don't shoot that in here," Pete stuck his face around Robert's wide back and warned them.

"Shut it Pete," Robert muttered out of the side of his mouth.

"Put it down buddy, that don't belong to you and let her go now," Tim gave the guy another chance.

"No, all of you put your guns down, now, or I'll shoot her," the skinny guy said and pointed the pistol into Ernestine's temple.

"Be calm Ernestine and don't move," Tim said to her evenly.

"I want my pistol," she grumbled and she pulled her hand up from the side of her leg where she was holding the 9mm still and where the skinny man hadn't seen it.

"I'll shoot her! Don't move!" he screeched and he jabbed her in the head with her own pistol again as he tightened his chokehold he had around her throat with his other arm.

His voice echoed in the cavernous room that was filled with liquid oxygen compressed into 25 foot tall tubes and caused everyone to jump a bit, but not Ernestine. She calmly but swiftly pulled her right arm across her body and pressed the muzzle against his upper thigh and squeezed off a round. At the same time Tim fired his big 30.06 which easily blasted through the man's chest and out the other side of him and then blew a hole in the tube of liquid oxygen right behind him.

Ernestine wrenched away from him and grabbed her little .38 out of his hand as he crumpled to the floor, his face white and his eyes squinched shut in pain.

"Mine!" she hissed.

"Ernestine get away from there!" Tim yelled at her and pulled her away from the stream of liquid oxygen gushing out in a white cloud straight down at the floor from where the ragged hole had been blasted in the tall canister.

Sirens blared throughout the facility and red lights began to flash at all the stairwells and this brought the heavy steps of the big man who had levelled Ernestine with one big swat. He came pounding down the stairs and he was not unarmed.

"Shit!" Robert yelled and tried to push Pete out of the way

because now Pete was stepping towards the leaking canister just as Tim was trying to pull Ernestine away from it.

"No!" Tim yelled as Pete raised his wavering arm with the fat red flare gun in it.

Tim tried to shove Ernestine away from the leak and onto the floor as Pete fired the flare gun and as the fat guy on the stairs raised his shotgun. The red streaming flare lit up the whole room like the inside of a volcano as it made its short arc towards the gushing, freezing liquid.

Robert spun around and jumped down the stairs four at a time to get to the second level just as Ernestine fired her pistol five fast pops at the fat man before she hit the floor with her shoulder from Tim's shove just as Pete's flare made contact with the leaking liquid oxygen. The whole room glared bright white before blossoming to red and then blasting them with heat and sound and sharp curved metal pieces blew through the air in a blast that was sound and light to which they closed their eyes against. The heat from the ceiling urged them to get up and go.

"Jesus, get up!" Tim cried but Ernestine couldn't really hear him. She could just see his sweaty face and his mouth working urgently and see blood trickling down in his eyes underneath the thick lenses of his glasses.

He pulled her up by her elbows and she found her feet and clamored down the stairs after Robert and though she knew her socked feet were hitting the stairs hard; she couldn't really feel them.

"Go go go! It's all going to blow!" Robert screamed as he opened the door for them. The incoming air from opening the door caused a soft whoosh to grow above them.

Robert grabbed Ernestine by her other elbow and helped Tim pull her across the parking lot to the other side of the big utility truck. When they got behind it, both men pulled her down on the ground.

Pete slid in behind them right on his backside, panting and screaming and freaking out in some sort of shock induced panic attack. But it was all drowned out as the rest of the tubes of liquid oxygen heated up and exploded one after another. They lay there on top of each other in a bundle on the ground, nearly crawling under the truck as blast after blast ripped open the night. When they thought it would never end, it finally did and Tim sat up first and peeked around the truck.

"Twenty-nine blasts, they all went up I think."

Ernestine sat up and felt hot sticky fluid flowing down the left side of her head. She couldn't hear anything but a loud high humming. She opened and closed her mouth several times as wide as she could and popped her jaw several times but did not succeed in popping her ears; in getting rid of the humming.

"Your ear is full of blood, don't touch it," Robert yelled in her face and she finally was able to hear him. "We'll fix it when we get home!" he assured her.

"Let's go before the cops or who the hell is in charge of the world now, comes," Tim beckoned to them from where he was heading back to the hedgerow from where they came.

Tim pulled Ernestine along the hedgerow but the cold damp weeds soaked her socks and then the shock really kicked in and she moved slower and slower until finally Robert just scooped her up and threw her over his shoulder and carried her like a sack of laundry. She suddenly felt sleepy and she let her eyes close for a just a little while. Just until she realized they were no longer traveling across soft squelching ground and just as she heard a familiar voice and smiled from where she hung over Robert's shoulder.

"Put the woman down, you pricks, and no one gets shot!"

CHAPTER SEVENTEEN

"Who the hell is that?" Robert asked and tightened his grip on Ernestine.

Ernestine opened her eyes and saw him standing there. His hair was longer than she remembered and his beard was bushier and wilder but it was him, even in the moonlight she could tell from here it was him; the defiant way he held himself, relaxed looking to those who didn't know him, but ready to spring underneath. She could tell it was him in how he had his rifle up to his shoulder and his cheek on the stock, eye to the sight, ready to go. He could stand like that forever and never waver. She knew his breathing would be slow and his pulse slower, even as he was ready to shoot.

"What part of that didn't you understand? You pricks," he said and sighted his rifle on Robert's knee and Ernestine knew they had two seconds to comply after that second warning.

"Ed," she said and raised her hand feebly and let it drop.

"Who is this asshole?" Robert asked.

Pete had taken to hiding behind Robert's wide girth again and was peering around at the man with the long dirty blonde hair and the beard; the man who had black wraparound sunglasses on in the night.

"Ed?" Tim asked and lowered his rifle. "Is that you?"

This question caused the blonde man to quickly target Tim with his rifle. He tightened his grip on the rifle and re-wrapped the strap he had around his hand and put his eye to the sight again.

"Dude, it's me, it's Tim Gray, from the gun shop."

"Tim?" the blonde man growled.

"Yes, calm the hell down, man, ease up. Lower your weapon."

But he didn't lower it. Now he swung it over to point at Robert once more. His back looked tense and his whole body was taut and leaning towards Robert.

"Tell that prick to put my wife down," the blonde man said between clenched teeth.

"Ex-wife," Ernestine muttered and shook her head slowly from where she was still hanging upside-down.

"You know this man?" Pete asked from behind Robert.

"It's Ed. It's my ex-husband," she said and tapped Robert and he slowly and gently let her down to the ground.

"Ugh," she groaned and swayed on her feet and held the side of her head which was bleeding heavier now from having been carried upside-down.

"Gotcha!" the blonde man rumbled as he stepped forward fast as a flash and grabbed Ernestine from around the waist.

"What are you pricks doing with my ex-wife?" he demanded and now he had the rifle hung over his shoulder on its strap and he had drawn a long .45 semi auto in his hand and was pointing it at them.

"They're friends," Ernestine said and leaned into him.

"All of them?" Ed asked.

"Yes."

"Even the weaselly one in the back?" he asked and waved the silver beast of a pistol towards Pete.

"Yes," she sighed. "They've been helping me."

"Let's get you home, Ernie," Ed said to her and pulled her arm over his shoulder and helped her hobble down the road of the trailer park, "before the cops get here," he added just as sirens screamed through the night as they barreled past the trailer park towards the water treatment facility.

"Keep the lights off," Ed told them as they went in the door of an old white and teal trailer around the corner from the one they had staked out as a retreat before rescuing Ernestine.

After they all got in the door, Ed locked it and double checked the wooden blinds that covered the windows on the door and the little windows in what was the narrow living room.

"We all need to be silent," he said to them with a quiet gravelly voice as he took his sunglasses off and slid them in his pocket. "Is everybody ok?" he asked and looked at each one as they nodded.

From outside they could hear more and more sirens screaming down the blacktop that went past the trailer park. Pete, Robert and Ernestine sat on the low velvet sofa while Tim stayed standing.

Ed squinted his eyes and looked from one of them to the next as if daring them to make a noise. His eyes lingered on Robert the longest and then finally they went back to Ernestine.

"Did you leave anyone alive?" he asked into the dark little room as he sat down in the big recliner that faced the tiny television set.

Ernestine squeezed her lips in a tight line and shook her head and as she did, she felt warm blood begin to flow down the side of her neck again.

Ed left the room and came back with a bath towel folded up in a small rectangle.

"Here, put it," he said and held it up to the side of her head.

She took the towel and pressed it to her ear just slightly and the pain caused her to snap her head back to the side away from it. There was glass or something sharp stuck in her ear and she could not apply pressure to it without wincing.

"Here, come back to the bathroom, there's no windows in there, we can turn on the light," Ed gestured to her and led her down to a short hall.

In the bathroom she passed by the mirror without looking in it yet still she couldn't avoid the blur of red blood she saw all down the left side of her pink jogging suit. She ignored it and didn't look closely at herself and sat down on the toilet lid.

"Let me take a look at that," Ed said to her, pulling a flashlight out of his pants pockets.

She let him look at her ear but when he tried to touch it, she reared back from him so hard she smacked the other side of her head into the wall.

"This place is tiny as shit," Ed chuckled quietly. "Stay still, you got metal bits in there I think. You should rinse your ear out," he told her and waved her over to the shower and gave her the handheld sprayer.

"Now, let me pick these out of your ear," he said when she was done spraying out her ear and had sat down on the counter of the sink.

She held still and silent as Ed picked out about twenty sharp little white metal shards that had embedded themselves in her ear; the lobe, the outside cartilage and even inside. He pulled them out gently but quickly and when they started bleeding all over again, he packed her ear with cotton balls and Neosporin and wrapped a bandage around her head. He was in the middle of wrapping the white batting around and around her dark head when suddenly he froze.

"Quiet," he said barely above a whisper and then tucked the tail of the bandage in and turned off the light. "Get in the tub, and lie down," he told her and she did.

But she also pulled out her 9mm and was ready for whatever he had heard. He flicked off the lights and stood silent and still next to the door and then he squatted down low.

Ernestine strained to hear with her non-bandaged ear but there was nothing till at last she heard, but more than that, she felt footsteps in the trailer. The men were moving quietly.

She saw bright light under the bathroom door when she peeked over the tub and then the roar of engines and spitting gravel caused her to jump. But she held her breath as she felt the trailer tilt and shake as the doors on both sides of the little domicile were wrenched open and the steps of many men coming in the tiny metal house vibrated through the bottom of the tub she was stretched out in.

"Hey hey hey, we're remainders," she heard Pete say. He was in the little hall, right outside their bathroom. She pictured him on his way to hide in the bedroom, but he hadn't made it.

"We have the right to be here," came from Tim.

"What are you doing sitting here in the dark?" a man's voice demanded.

"We heard sirens! We heard an explosion!" Robert cried out in an innocent sounding voice that Ernestine gave him credit for.

"How did you even know we were here?" Tim asked.

"Shut up and hands on the wall!"

There were sounds of scuffling and grunting. Someone kicked the wall five times in a row and cursed and kicked again and the whole trailer shook and then a door banged open. Ernestine strained to hear from where she still lay in the tub and could just make out retreating boots and then silence.

She peeked out of the tub at Ed but he was standing up again and so still with his back to her that she didn't even dare to breathe in very loudly. She waited for him to say something. After what seemed forever, after her side and her shoulder were completely numb from lying in the tub, Ed finally cracked open the door of the bathroom and looked out in the hall. He had his shiny nickel coated pistol out again; the one he had always kept in the side table drawer when they had lived together.

Ernestine pulled herself up out of the tub, touching her bandaged ear as she went, and followed Ed into the little living room.

"What kind of firepower do you have?" he asked her as he felt around on a low coffee table till he found his cigarettes in the semidark room.

Ernestine heard the familiar crinkle of cellophane and waited until he struck his match to speak up.

"I have my Ruger," she said and held out her 9mm that Tim had returned to her in the water treatment plant. "And I have my .38 but it's empty."

"Nice, been shopping without me I see," Ed chuckled and then said, "All right sit down," he pointed to the couch as he held his glowing cigarette in his mouth. "I'll be right back."

Ed gave her three magazines for the 9mm and he had a box of .38s and one speed loader.

"What the hell are with these pants, Ernie? There's no pockets."

She was fiddling around with the waistband of the pants, trying to find a place to put everything but there was nowhere.

"It's a long story."

Ed went back to the bedroom and she could hear him digging around for a minute in his closet.

"Here," he said and threw her a pair of folded black cotton pants with cargo pockets down the sides onto the couch next to her.

"Who's are these?" Ernestine asked, her voice going shrill.

Ed shrugged, "A girlfriend from a long time ago."

"Libby?"

"Naw, two or three after her."

Ernestine took the pants grudgingly and went to the bathroom and changed into them. They were fresh and clean and a nice change from the kitten pants she'd been wearing almost six days. Ed knocked on the door and gave her a worn, soft black t-shirt and said, "That's mine," as she took it and shut the door.

There was dried blood all over her shoulder and neck and she rubbed at it with the dirty sweatshirt before pulling on the t-shirt Ed had gave her.

"I still don't have shoes," she said as she peeled the wet socks off her feet.

"Libby didn't leave any of those," he laughed. "Don't worry, my neighbor is about your size, we can break in there and get you some."

"All right, holster your handguns, Ernie," Ed said to her and handed her more gear.

Ernestine tucked in the baggy black t-shirt and then filled her pockets with ammo. She buckled the shoulder holster Ed had given her and slid in her .38.

"Now you need something with more range, more power, you want Old Faithful?" he asked her.

Old Faithful. She hadn't shot that in a long time. Old Faithful was a lever action .44 mag rifle that Ed had. It had always made Ed laugh because Ernestine could hit anything with it; a small Pringles lid hanging off a branch, a tennis ball, whatever, even at 200 yards or more. Ed won a lot of bets off Ernestine's skill with the Old Faithful, the model 92 rifle. Men usually thought little Ernestine wouldn't be able to handle the kick, but she knew how to hold it just right and she was a dead aim every single time. But that had been years ago.

"Sure I'll take Old Faithful," she said after a second of thinking and then, "What are you taking?"

"The Blackout," he stated; his voice papery and dry. "With the suppressor."

"That doesn't have much range."

"That's what I have you for. We'll just have to hope you can still shoot worth a damn. Now let's get you some shoes and get those douchebags back and see who's in charge these days."

"Is there anybody even there?" Ernestine asked Ed from where they squatted in a thick mass of cattails and six inches of water leaking into her stolen Jordans she had swiped from one of Ed's neighbors.

They had been squatting there for over ten minutes watching black SUV and after black SUV leave the facility, quietly, but with their lights still turning in red and blue circles, till there was only one black sedan left.

Smoke roiled thick above the facility and the smell of burning shit was thick in their noses. Ernestine couldn't believe the building was still standing.

"Somebody's there," was all Ed would say.

They waited another five minutes to see if that somebody would leave and then they got tired of waiting and decided to go in.

"Let's go in a different way than we did," Ernestine suggested.

"Why so?"

"Because I'm fairly certain we blew that way up entirely," she muttered and her hand went voluntarily up to her bandaged ear.

They ran around to the other side of the building and found a locked door that led down into a basement.

"It's a no go," Ed said as they tried it.

"Window, up there," Ernestine pointed to the transom that was open above a window that was protected by a wire cage. "Hoist me up there," she told Ed as she ran over to it.

Ed cupped his hands and hoisted Ernestine up as high as he could.

"It's a good thing you're still small," he panted as his arms shook as she pushed off his palm with her foot and clambered up on top of the wire cage around the window and then shimmied into the open transom.

"I'll let you in," was the last thing she said before dropping to the other side with a muffled kerflump.

Ed's thing was to listen. His vision wasn't so great but he could hear and he had great intuition so Ernestine was silent once she let him in and she waited as he stood and listened in the dark basement hallway. And then she followed him down the gloomy tiled hall to the end to a staircase leading up.

"We go up," he said, "we go up quietly but fast."

She followed her ex-husband up the stairs and on each landing they paused and listened till they had gone up five flights.

"This one," was all he said and they ran down another hall and stopped, each of them on opposite sides of an open door.

Ernestine could hear the staccato click of high heels on a hard cement floor walking stiffly back and forth across a large room. She peered around the lip of the door to see what was happening and she saw Pete, Robert, and Tim all on their knees with their hands bound behind their backs and their wrists bound to their ankles by a short rope. They had gags in their mouths and Pete's glasses were missing and she could see that one of his eyes was swollen shut. She could only see the sides of their faces as the woman in the high heels paced back and forth in front of them.

"Do you recognize her?" Ed asked as Ernestine ducked back behind the edge of the door.

"No."

"Ugly enough," Ed said and looked at the woman again.

She had blonde hair cut in a ragged thin bob that framed her stern angry face. The bottom of her jaw jutted out like a bulldog's and the red lipstick accentuated her mean mouth. Her eyes were small and heavily lined with black eyeliner and Ernestine wondered who would put make-up and high heels on in the middle of the night when the whole world seemed to have gone to shit.

"Well," the woman said and pursed her thin lips as she looked at the men on their knees in front of her. "This is unfortunate," she said and smiled, showing her small teeth, "but I don't like interruptions in my plans," and then she raised her arm that was holding a big semiautomatic pistol with a suppressor on the end of it and pointed it at Tim and shot him with a silent swoosh right in the chest.

"Jesus!" Ernestine whispered under her own hand and flattened herself against the wall before peeking out again.

Robert and Pete had flinched away so hard from Tim being shot that they had fallen over on their sides and looked like two bound shrimp curled up on the floor. Men in black pants and shirts stepped out of the dark shadows and set them back up on their knees as Tim lay motionless on his side, blood pumping out a small neat hole in the front of his shirt; his eyes squeezed shut and a grimace still on his face around the gag in his mouth. It took two men to set Robert back up on his knees and it took one to keep Pete up, because Pete's body kept trying to crumple from the shock he'd just received, from what he'd just seen.

"There's at least ten of them," Ed told her, his face emotionless as he counted how many men he saw behind Pete and Robert.

"What are we going to do?" Ernestine asked.

"Shh, she's talking."

"This facility is under the control of federal government now and you are all guilty of treason, I believe," she said as she held one finger to her mouth and rolled her eyes as if thinking about something.

She paced back and forth a few more times, her shiny high heels clicking on the hard polished cement floor. She held her head high as she strutted back and forth in her tight black skirt and matching jacket. Her wide butt strained the cheap material as she went and she smiled and winked at a big black man standing behind Robert.

"We need to draw them away from here," Ed said as he crept away from the door and back to the stairwell.

"What are you-" Ernestine tried to ask what he was going to do but he was gone already; disappeared down the black stairs.

Ernestine went back to the door where she had been and watched the woman pacing once again. She hoped she didn't shoot anyone else; it was hard to not shoot her for killing Tim but there were too many men there with her. Ernestine couldn't possibly take them all on. She hoped Ed hurried with whatever it was he was doing.

"I don't like people who meddle. I don't like people who don't follow the group plan. I don't like people who get in the way nor do I like people who think they're clever," the high heeled woman said and stopped right in front of Pete with a sneer on her ugly mouth.

"You," she said and then did a quick fake smile down at Pete who was squinting up at her through one eye. "You think you're clever, don't you? You would have been fine. We would have let you be even though you were supposed to be relocated and even though you remained. We know there's more of you in this little group," she said and waved the long pistol around and walked over to Robert.

Two large men came up behind Robert as if to hold him in place yet they didn't get that close to him. Maybe they were afraid of getting shot by her accidentally if they got too close.

"You," she said and smiled at Robert and brought up her arm slowly to point the gun at him but then she stopped.

She stopped. She paused. She sniffed the air and as she did several heads turned and looked at the door on the opposite wall from where Ernestine was hiding. Smoke was drifting up into the room from what must have been another stairwell.

"What is on fire now?" the woman demanded with almost a shriek and lowered her weapon.

The men in black all looked together as one at the gray smoke that was now swirling into the room, but they stood still and didn't move.

"Go and find out what it is!" she screamed and stomped one of her feet.

Ernestine watched as all ten of the men filed into the stairwell and clanged down the stairs that she couldn't see. She hoped Ed was ready for them all because now there was no turning back.

Ernestine stepped out from her shadowy hiding place and into the room silently and raised her Ruger at the woman in the tight black skirt. The woman heard Pete as he let out a garbled cry of excitement at seeing Ernestine as she came in. The woman in the tight skirt whipped around to see what the commotion was all about and when her eyes spotted Ernestine they widened in surprise and anger and color flooded her pockmarked face and she raised her own pistol as she started to scream at Ernestine.

But a long suppressor changes the motion of raising a pistol; it adds six or seven inches to the gun and makes for a longer raising time. It throws the shooter, who has always practiced shooting with their normal gun, off balance, and in this case it gave Ernestine, who already had a few seconds of lead time on the woman, a few more seconds to react.

"Shut it, you bitch!" Ernestine hissed quietly, and maybe she was the only one who heard it, but everyone heard her double tap, her two fast shots, blam! Blam! At the woman in the black skirt. But the first shot went wide and hit the woman in her right shoulder and spun her around slightly and the second shot went lower than the first and hit her in the side of her hip, and the woman crumpled, screaming.

Ernestine strode up to the woman and kicked her pistol away from her blood-drenched hand and picked it up. Its grips were huge and flared and the checkering was aggressive and felt wrong in Ernestine's hand and she took it over to Robert and laid it down by his knees. As she began to pull at the tape around Robert's wrists, she felt five growing explosions, each one louder than the first, vibrate through the concrete under her knees.

"We have to go!" yelled Ed as he came flying back up the stairs where Ernestine and him had been hiding before he left to create a diversion. His face was black and his hair looked singed.

Ed slid into the room on his boots and went down on his knees and began slicing the tape away from Pete while Ernestine pulled out a knife and started cutting Robert free, and then she looked at the woman as she lay bleeding on the floor.

"You didn't kill her?" Ed asked Ernestine as he frowned at the woman who was now writhing on the floor as blood pumped out of the side of her thigh.

She only shook her head no.

"You didn't use Old Faithful?"

She shook her head again.

"Oh well, let's get out of here," Ed said and helped pull Pete to his feet.

"Where are we gonna go?" Pete asked.

"Well, we can't go to my house and we can't go to yours; they'll know about both of those places," Ed said grimly.

Ernestine looked down at Tim's body. There was a red bloom that started at his chest and went all the way to his waist where his shirt was tucked in. She looked at his face which was now relaxed around the gag in his mouth and his eyes looked peacefully closed. But then she saw a snot bubble expand out of his nose and pop and then she heard his ragged, wet breathing through his clogged nose and she leaned over and yanked his gag off.

"I know where we can go. And we need to go now," she gasped as she flicked open her knife again.

She began to cut the ties on Tim's wrists as the men looked on.

CHAPTER EIGHTEEN

"We'll get there," Ed said from where he sat at the wheel of Tim's loud truck as it bounced further and further away from town.

Ernestine kept turning around and looking behind them as they went. The truck sounded ominously loud out on the dark country road. But all she saw behind them was Robert at the wheel of his truck and behind him, Pete at the wheel of Ernestine's Prius. Tim was in the back hatch of the Prius with both seats folded flat so he could stretch out.

He had come awake when they were halfway back to the trailer park; their second trip from the water plant that night back past the dog park, through the marsh and the weeds. He had come awake half way home as they were carrying him. He cried and groaned all the way to the car and so they ran faster because they could not get him to be quiet.

They had put him in the back of the Prius immediately and Ernestine had applied pressure and a bandage while Ed and Robert ran back to his trailer and retrieved all of Ed's guns in a wheelbarrow. That's how many he had. And that was how many steel boxes of ammo he had too. Robert was carrying an enormous duffel bag full of supplies and Ed was wheeling the wheelbarrow. Tim was talking calmer once the bandage was on and once he could lay down in the back of the small car and could sip some water. He even gave a thumbs up when Ernestine left him to get in the truck with Ed. Ed had taken one look at the pistol Ernestine had gotten off the lady and said it was just a .22 and that Tim would be fine. He gave it no other thought and Ernestine remembered his shortness with things and how it had irritated her when they were married.

But she hoped he was right, and she turned around and faced the road as Ed took a sharp turn onto a narrow road right in to the middle of the Shawnee Forest. It was a rocky dirt road only one lane wide and if you didn't know where it was in the tree line, you would drive right past it. But Ed knew where it was just as he knew where his own nose was on his own face.

"I can't believe we left them all alive," Ed finally said just as they crossed a very narrow and high bridge over the wide dark lake deep in the forest.

Ernestine could hear frogs and crickets mindlessly singing in every direction in the dark and she chose to listen to them and not Ed. But he wouldn't be quiet.

"I can't believe we didn't like, blow that place apart or something or blaze it to the ground with those tanks I blew up. That place is built like a brick shithouse. And that's what it is, when you think about it."

Still she didn't say anything and Ed popped open a cold can of Pepsi he had brought with and then he passed it to Ernestine who realized she was very thirsty and also extremely hungry. She couldn't remember her last meal.

"I can't believe we left all the food and water and supplies back at my house. I have tons of food and a tent and clean clothes and a coat and just everything. My computer. My purse. My cellphone. I need to get in touch with my mom," she said to Ed but he didn't answer for a long time.

"We can go back in a few days and clear it out, but it's probably being staked out," he finally said.

"You think those people won't let this go?"

"No. No way."

Ernestine sighed and leaned her head back on the seat but the road was too bumpy for her to get relaxed and rest.

"Just a few more miles," Ed said and shook a cigarette out his pack and lit it and blew the smoke out the window as he wound them deeper and deeper into the forest.

The trees above were now so thick that they shut off the sky and even blocked out the moonlight. Ernestine felt closed in and stuck her forehead out the open window and breathed in the night air.

"Enjoy the air while you can because that little trailer of Tim's is gonna be packed tight like a bitch," Ed warned her and then flicked his cigarette out into the night.

Ernestine watched it bounce in the rearview mirror until the truck with Robert hulking behind the wheel drove over it and then she watched it roll and spark off into the ditch before the Prius could drive over it. And as they went up a steep hill she looked at the black ribbon of road behind them and saw that no one followed them for as far as she could see.

To be continued.

Made in the USA
Monee, IL
25 May 2020

31868304R00118